PAKHAN'S SECRET BABY

KRYSTAL CLARK

Copyright © 2025 by Krystal Clark

All rights reserved.

No part of this book may be reproduced in any form or by any electronic or mechanical means, including information storage and retrieval systems, without written permission from the author, except for the use of brief quotations in a book review.

ONE

Leo

IT HAS BEEN MORE than ten years since I last saw her smile.

Even now, she's not smiling. Her lips, painted a deep shade of crimson, are set in a tense line.

The crystalline glow from the chandeliers sketches patterns of light on the swell of her breasts. Since she gave birth ten years ago, her figure has stayed luscious and full. She now has curves everywhere, and it's hard to look away.

"Leo, what a surprise to see you." Irritation flickers in my forehead when Anatoly Popov, an oligarch I saved last year from the Sokolov syndicate's schemes, greets me. Anatoly and I aren't friends, but we're allies. He is more than willing to let me use his political and social connections in return for continued protection from his enemies in the underworld. "I thought you were in Las Vegas."

"I wouldn't miss your daughter's engagement for anything."

I tip my head toward the center of the room. All the guests are dressed opulently, but one couple stands out even among the guests. "You must be so proud. Your daughter chose an exceptional man."

Anatoly beams at his daughter and son-in-law, who are glittering in fine clothes. They're the perfect Russian couple. Both blonde, both tall and beautiful. Educated and rich. Upper-class. Like twins, who were born into different families, destined to be united.

"People like them belong together." My thoughts turn into absentminded words. I've always wondered: how do some people end up finding and falling in love with someone just like them? Someone suitable for them in every way. Attainable. An easy love like that could never be mine.

Anatoly laughs, oblivious to the bitterness burning my tongue. "I'll tell my daughter you think she and her husband are meant to be."

I smile, gazing beyond the blissful couple to the woman who is standing with a tense face. Years of pent-up longing, anger, desire, and regret collide into a massive supernova inside my chest.

Anya is here with her husband. After years of not seeing each other, why did it have to be now?

We are as different as chalk and cheese, destined to never be together.

My hair is a dirty, dark brown streaked with silver, my eyes the biting gray of a Siberian winter sky.

Her hair is the perfect shade of gold, and her eyes are soft blue, like she was picked out of a Hans Christian Anderson fairytale.

She's a former ballerina and figure skater, and I'm a gangster.

She married a man who was suited for her. Just like Popov's daughter.

Her husband's arm curves around her hips. She stiffens, muscles protruding through the skin on her neck.

Igor Petrov's reputation is terrible, both as a husband and a politician. He has been in a few bribery scandals, but with the help of his connections and family's wealth, he has clung to his position. He has supporters in the Kremlin, that's for sure. There have been rumors forever that his relationship with Anya is rocky, but she never comments on it. I haven't seen her in nearly a decade now. We never moved in the same circles. Her husband isn't one of my allies.

But he looks just like her. Polished, elegant. Normal. There's no air of danger around him. He isn't made of half muscle and half vengeance. One would expect a famous skater like her to end up with someone respectable and powerful like him.

The world is very predictable. People marry people like themselves. Opposites attract, but they also burn out like the ashes left behind by a dying flame.

"Oh, do you know her? Anya Petrova?" Anatoly raises his eyebrows.

I shake my head. "Nyet. She looks like someone I used to know."

That's right. I used to know Anya Vasilieva, a bright-eyed, sixteen-year-old girl with a fondness for piroshky. I knew the young woman Anya Vasilieva, who shocked the world with her stunning athletic ability and made a name for herself in the competitive world of figure skating. I remember Anya, the gold medalist, the woman who sought raw passion at the cusp of marriage as she came apart under me and her pussy clenched around my cock.

I don't know Anya Petrova. She's a stranger.

"Do you want me to introduce you to Petrov?" Anatoly inquires when I continue staring at Anya. "He isn't affiliated with anyone in the bratva, as far as I know. He might be open to an offer. He has been having a hard time."

I swallow, feeling copper coat my tongue. The last thing I want is an alliance with Anya's husband.

"Aren't there rumors about him being a philanderer?" My lip curls in distaste. "Will he be able to keep his seat?"

Anatoly claps his hands together. "When has cheating ever been enough to ruin a Russian politician's career?"

"He doesn't seem powerful." I know he isn't.

"Well, he has some influence over the port in St. Petersburg. He could ease some troubles for you."

Even so, I don't want to get friendly with him. Because that would mean seeing Anya more often. I've done everything to avoid her for nine years now.

Being around her makes my cold, frozen heart feel like it's still dying. Decaying, rotting with agony.

I should have forgotten about her, but I never will. Now that my brothers have all provided heirs and the succession of my pakhan title is assured, I'm even less inclined to think about marrying another woman. Not that I could ever marry Anya, anyway. I mean, I could kill her husband, but nowadays I avoid unnecessary bloodshed.

Anatoly tilts his head at me, silently asking me to follow him. I do so reluctantly.

A few strides later, I'm standing next to the woman I never stopped loving. And that's clear because my heart is trashing against my ribcage like someone shocked it back to life.

Anya looks up, her eyes like the calmest blue sea. But the moment she sees me, they narrow. Her pupils dilate.

I like that I still have an effect on her, even if it's mostly fear now. I know her secrets. I have the ability to ruin her. Maybe she's scared I will do it.

"Petrov, meet Leo Antonov. He's a very influential man." Anatoly introduces me. I make small talk with her husband as Anya stays by his side, unmoving, a very fake smile pasted to her lips.

Anya pulls her gaze away from me as a young boy, around ten years old, clings to her, coming up silently from behind her.

Anya takes his hand, stroking his knuckles and then his hair. "Aleksandr," she whispers.

It's her son. Aleksandr Petrov. Ten years old.

He looks up at me with innocent blue eyes. Just like his mother's.

He has brown hair, even though both his parents have blonde hair.

I have a theory about that.

Anya holds the boy close to her side, as if she's afraid I'll kidnap him.

She's nervous. That's clear from the way her chest rises dramatically every time she breathes. Her breasts, rounded and bigger after pregnancy and motherhood, press through her plunging neckline. My cock twitches.

Anya Petrova looks like a sexy siren, even though she's over forty. Once, she was slim and graceful. She had the figure of a ballerina and the face of a fairy. But now she has the figure of a woman who has been shaped by age. Maternal, filled out in all the right places. Her curves add to her sex appeal. My fingers warm from the need to touch her, to squeeze her perfect tits and hear her raspy cries.

They still echo inside my head sometimes at night when I can't sleep.

"This is my wife, Anya." Petrov's voice barely registers through the chaotic emotions twisting in my chest.

My groin clenches. Warmth floods my stomach as Anya raises her hand to shake mine. I take her hand, feeling its softness for the first time in nearly a decade.

I brush my thumb over her knuckles, listening for the subtle catch in her breath. She rewards me with the sweetest moan, so low that only I hear it.

"Nice to meet you, Mr. Antonov." Her voice is careful. She wants to pretend that we're strangers. I don't blame her for it. How would she explain our acquaintance to her husband? Or tell him that I was the one she came to on her wedding night when she discovered Petrov's first infidelity. I was the one who carried her in my arms like a bride after she had married another man. I was the one fucked her raw on her marriage night. I was the one who made her come twice. Made her sob with pleasure and forget all about the bastard who had broken her heart.

But I'll never be her husband or the man she chooses to be with.

Blood rushes between my legs instantly when she tries to take her hand away. I hold on tighter, asserting my strength for no reason other than to let her know I still can.

"And this is my son." Petrov pushes Aleksandr toward me. I find his treatment of his son odd. He should be treating the boy like a future political prince, not shoving him like he's an unwanted orphan.

"What a cute boy," I say in a droll voice, stroking the child's hair. I brush his head. A few strands of his hair stick to my hands. I take my hand away and bury it in my pocket. "You must be so proud to have a boy like him."

"He's not very smart. Must take after his mother." Petrov guffaws.

"He is still young," Anya says defensively. "And he has been doing well with his new tutor."

"I never had tutors at his age," Petrov criticizes. "Did you, Popov?"

Anatoly looks awkward, caught between husband and wife. "Well, it was different when we were young. We didn't need to compete for jobs in the Soviet Union. They say it's harder now. Globalization has changed the landscape."

Petrov grunts, unconvinced. "So, Mr. Antonov, what kind of business do you run?"

I straighten. "It's a conglomerate. With headquarters in Russia and the United States. But we have operations in other parts of Europe, too."

"Sounds promising." There's a glint in Petrov's eye. I can sense his greed. He knows I'm rich, and he wants to see how it can benefit him. "I know many businessmen. I'm a supporter of big businesses. I'm always keen to help Russian corporations. If you have any ideas, don't hesitate to tell me."

I don't want to give him a dime. I never want to see him again. But knowing a politician is always useful.

"If you're free later this week, we can have dinner. It's too noisy to discuss anything here." I grit my teeth as some of the bride's friends cheer for her.

That's followed by the announcement that dinner is ready and the guests may proceed to the dining hall.

"You're right. Here's my card." Petrov thrusts a card with his number at me. I take it and smile at him.

I don't need to follow up on my words.

I pull back. "I can't stay for dinner. I have business," I tell Anatoly.

He nods in understanding. "I'll see you again at my daughter's wedding, then."

I turn around. My phone has been buzzing, but I couldn't take the call while being in public surrounded by civilians. One never knows who is listening.

My legs eat up the space with fast strides as I move out of the building and into the parking lot. I answer the call.

"What's wrong, Igor?"

"The cocaine shipment from Mexico has been delayed, boss."

That's not a major issue. We don't have anybody counting on us to get that shipment into Russia on time. We will be able to sell the drugs and make money even if it comes in a few days later. I'll just have to let my men at the port know.

"I'll talk to them," I say. "See if they can do something about it."

"I already talked to them. The local police seized their goods."

"So they won't be able to supply us?" I ask, frowning.

"They say they have more of the product, but it's in Norway. We'll have to help them move the goods to St. Petersburg."

I rub my temples. "That will cost us money. Customs in Europe are a pain. I'll renegotiate the price with the Mexican supplier. I'll probably be able to bring it down by quite a bit. Can they still supply the same quantity they promised?"

"I'm not certain."

"Alright. I'll ask them. Leave this to me, Igor. You keep an eye on the situation in Las Vegas. I don't want trouble with American authorities again."

"Yes, Boss."

The parking lot breathes cold. Exhaust ghosts drift under yellow lamps, the asphalt slick with a thin skin of frost. Music from the banquet hall thumps through the concrete like a distant heartbeat. I pocket my phone and turn, already calculating the next call, when silk and perfume halt me.

Anya stands a few paces away with her son tucked into her side. She is all pale light and red mouth, a winter saint in a dress that should be outlawed. The boy wriggles free and jogs toward a puddle that mirrors the chandelier glow spilling from the entry doors.

My eyes narrow. I realize she must have heard part of the call. She must know what I was talking about.

As if reading my mind, her hands come up over her chest. "Don't worry. I won't tell anyone what I heard."

My frown stays where it is. "Good," I say. "I would hate to see the Popovs' party turn into a federal raid."

A breath escapes her, almost a laugh, almost a sound of pain. "You have not changed. You're still giving orders and being...what you were."

"Neither have you." I let my gaze sweep her slowly, greedy and cruel. "Except here." I gesture to the soft fullness of her breasts where crystal light pools. "And here." The lines that bracket her mouth. "Time was kind."

Her hand lifts like a shield, fingers brushing the corner of her jaw.

"The gray hair surprised me," she murmurs, pointing at my head. "You were a young man last time we...saw each other. It made me realize we are older now."

"Older," I agree. "Not dead."

Her eyes flare. The boy darts between cars, shoes tapping the wet. She follows him with a mother's precise attention, then brings her gaze back to me. "Are you going to dinner?"

"No. I have somewhere to be. You should go. Your husband already went to the dining hall with Popov. I thought you were with him."

She inhales loudly. "Aleksandr was feeling suffocated inside. Too many people. He wanted some air, so I came out with him."

She hesitates, rubbing her ear. It's a habit of hers. She does that when she's anxious. She used to do it all the time before a competition, before she had to perform a set.

"With your... business," Anya says the last word as if it tastes like iron. "Are you still doing the same thing?"

"I'm a pakhan," I answer. "That is not a job I can quit." The words scrape. I add what has lived under my tongue for years. "Isn't that why you left me?"

Her lips part. The old heat rises like smoke between us, hot and bitter.

"I left," she says, "because I wanted simple things. A house without locks, mornings without blood on the news, a safe home for the family I dreamed of having." Her eyes harden. "You cannot give me that."

I step closer. Cold peels off the ground and climbs my legs. "I could have given you everything."

"Except safety," she says softly.

Silence stretches. Her son whoops at something only ten-year-old boys can see.

"You look gorgeous," I say, because honesty feels like violence. "Your husband must hate that."

This time, she laughs, real and quick. "He says I look like a fat, middle-aged woman." She lifts one shoulder. "He likes blondes who are twenty-two and slim. I used to look like that once. I suppose that's why he married me."

"Does he still cheat?"

Anya's mouth smooths into something sad. "He will never change."

Anger rises under my collar like a noose. "Don't you ever think of leaving him?"

"I have nowhere to go." She watches her son loop back toward us. "My parents died. My aunt and uncle are old. I have a child. I cannot take care of him alone."

"So you stay because it is convenient." Anger rages through my throat. "Because it is easy."

Her head snaps. "Nothing about staying is easy." Her voice is quiet and very even.

She doesn't offer more information, and I don't even want to know. Everything she says only raises my blood pressure. I hate that she's loyal to a man who gives her a worse life than I could have given her.

I hate that I'm not that man.

Aleksandr crouches to pry a pebble out of the crack in the asphalt. I look at his profile, the stubborn chin that looks like it does not belong to Petrov's bloodline. Something ugly and bright twists behind my ribs. I brush the inside of my pockets where strands of the boy's hair are stuck to my wool coat. I intend to use those to find out the truth. Anya would never tell me, but I've had my doubts since the moment I saw her son.

"Do you plan to do business with him?" she asks.

"I haven't decided yet."

"I wouldn't mind if you did," she says. "I might see you more often."

Her statement makes my heart pound furiously.

"Is seeing me not painful?"

"Not at all." She tucks a curl behind her ear, a gesture so old my body reacts before my brain catches up. "We were friends once."

"We were never friends." I step into her light. Her breath stirs against my throat. "We were lovers."

Color rises high in her cheeks. "Yeah, wild, passionate lovers. I miss my youth," she says, almost teasing, almost begging the past to return.

Then she smiles. It is the first time I have seen it in a decade, and it knocks something loose in me.

For a moment, it's as if all the time between us is gone, and we're back to being teenagers, back to smiling and laughing over silly things. How could I have known back then what would happen?

"You look good when you smile," I tell her. "Even with the lines."

"Even with." Her eyes brighten and then dim. "How is your life these days, Leo?"

"Efficient," I say. "Dangerous. Satisfactory." Lies that are also true. "Yours?"

"My son is all that keeps me alive." Her hand crosses to her ribs, protective, instinctive. "I want him to grow up happy and safe."

The message is clear. A man like me is neither of those things. I nod once. She's trying to tell me to stay away from her boy and her life.

Aleksandr abandons his pebble and sprints back, breath puffing. He skids to a stop, stares up at me with blue eyes that have haunted my worst nights. There's a flicker of recognition in him that he cannot place, that drags my chest tight. I guess he remembers me because he saw me just a few minutes ago.

"Time to go inside," Anya tells him in Russian, gentle and firm. "Two more minutes, Aleksandr."

He watches me for another heartbeat, then bolts away again. I drag my gaze from the boy and back to the woman who buried me and resurrected me in the same lifetime.

"I should go," I say.

She nods. "Goodnight, Leo."

"Goodnight, Anya."

I turn and cross the lot. The Bentley unlocks with a low click. Leather and cold air swallow me as I drop into the driver's seat and shut the door. My hands find the wheel out of habit. I close my eyes for a second, just long enough to taste regret, then open them to glass.

A small fist taps the window.

Through the glass, I see the visage of Anya's son. His cheeks are pink from the cold, contrasting starkly against his pale skin.

"What do you want?" I ask irately.

"Mr. Popov said you are a powerful man. More powerful than my papa," the boy answers, his eyes twinkling. "Is that true?"

I lower the glass. Cold knives in.

"Da." My voice is rougher than it should be. "You want my autograph?"

He shakes his head, serious now, the way serious looks on a child who has learned how to listen for footsteps. "Not your autograph. Something else."

"My business card? I'm sorry, but I don't have one," I say drily. I have never been great with kids, but this one does intrigue me. Not a lot of kids would chase after a man who looks like me. Huge, with tattoos that are barely hidden by my nice suit. Even a kid like him should sense that I'm trouble.

Aleksandr grips the edge of the window with both hands. Up close, he is a perfect echo of her eyes and a stranger's mouth. "I want help."

"What kind of help?"

"Help my mama leave my papa."

The world narrows to the shape of his small mouth, making those words. My fingers lock on the wheel. "Does your mama want to leave your papa?"

Hope flares in my chest, but I know it's pointless. Anya told me herself just now that she has no problem staying in a convenient marriage. I sensed something under the calm surface of her expression, something she wasn't telling me.

Is there something more to it?

Aleksandr comes closer to me, then falters. "She says we have nowhere. She says we are fine. We are not."

"Would you be all right if they divorced?"

He chews on the inside of his cheek. "Yes."

"Why do you think your mama should leave?" The question comes quietly. My heart is hammering, but my voice lands softly, so he keeps talking.

His eyes get glassy and furious at once. "Because my papa hits my mama."

Something inside me splits. Red spills through my vision, hot and cold at the same time. I feel each beat in my palms like an old injury waking.

"Who told you that word?" My voice barely crawls out.

"I saw." He swallows, and the sound is small. "He says sorry. He gives flowers. Then he is angry again."

"Does your Mama know you saw?"

He blinks, as if he's unsure of how to answer my question. "Don't tell her I told you. Please."

A second tap of footsteps blankets his breath. Anya appears at the corner of the hood, breathless. She takes in the tableau, her son with his hands on my car and me with my window down, and her face drains.

"Aleksandr," she says, gentle warning threaded with worry. "Inside now."

"Mama, please."

"Aleksandr." Her palm lifts toward him.

He looks at me, all stubborn hope. "Mr. Popov said you can do anything."

I could lie. I could tell him yes and make a promise that breaks three lives. I look past him to Anya. The porch light behind her crowns her hair in tame fire. Fear sits in her shoulders. Not of me. Of what truths set loose can cost.

"Go with your mama," I say at last, voice steady. "We will talk again."

His mouth tightens with a courage I recognize from the mirror I no longer look into. He releases the door and trots to Anya. She gathers him in with one arm. For a single ungodly second, her eyes meet mine over his head. They are wet and raging.

I lift the window. The glass slides up, severing the air between us. The engine turns over, a low growl. My hands shake once and then go still, the way they do before a decision I cannot take back.

Power means nothing unless it is used.

TWO

Anya

TWENTY-SIX YEARS AGO...

THE RINK SMELLS like cold metal and lemon soap. It's always brighter than I expect, the lights throwing glitter over the scratched ice.

I inhale. I love it here. I loved ballet first, the pink shoes and the quiet rooms and the endless mirrors, but skating took over my heart the first time I felt my blades bite and slide. I'm faster here. Freer. I can breathe.

I moved to Moscow two years ago when I started winning everything in our region. Papa said it was a waste to stay in our small town if I had a chance at something big. Mama cried, but she packed my sweaters and my lucky scarf and told me to skate like I was born to do it. My coach says I have a real shot this season. Russian Junior Nationals first, then maybe the

"Do you even have what it takes?" I tease, hands on my hips.

He gives me a look that would set lesser girls on fire. "I've done things you wouldn't be able to do."

"Yeah. Like what?"

He goes silent, then says it so soft I almost miss it. "Held a knife while someone begged. Cleaned a floor that wasn't dirty with dirt." He doesn't look at me. "My father said I should learn what it costs to win."

My stomach flips. I want to throw up and hug him at the same time. "I'm sorry," I whisper. "I'm sorry your papa is like that."

He shrugs, but it's the kind of shrug that says he feels it everywhere. "It is what it is."

"It doesn't have to be." I push my blade through a tiny arc. "You can choose different. You can choose to be a successful figure skater and leave that world behind."

His eyes come back to mine. A thread of something new pulls tight between us. Curiosity. Maybe faith. Maybe nothing. I can't tell yet.

"Maybe you're right." A slight smile curls at the corner of his lips. He looks breathtaking when he smiles. My heart pounds. I made a boy smile. "I feel hopeful now."

"Come on," I say, brighter, because if I sink we'll both drown. "Watch me. Sometimes that helps."

He gets off the ice and leans on the rail, arms folded, tattoo lines dark against his skin. I skate. I mean I really skate. Warm-up laps turn into run-throughs. I land my double axel like I promised my coach I would. I string a combination that's been killing me since Tuesday. The music inside my head gets louder than the rink's speakers. For a minute I'm not a girl from a small town living in a dorm with other girls who hate me. I'm a blade and a heartbeat and a line carved through white.

"What do you want, then?"

He stares at the ice. For a second he's so young my heart hurts. His expression is dejected and vulnerable. He reminds me of myself when I lose a competition. "I don't have dreams."

I hate that. I hate it so much I lean close like proximity will fix it. "Then borrow mine. We can share."

He blinks. "Your dream is what? Gold medals and a crown?"

"My dream is to skate clean programs and not cry when they read the scores. To be brave when it counts. To make something beautiful. Maybe win."

He considers that like I said the secret to the universe. "Winning doesn't sound bad," he admits. "I could try. Stand near you while you win."

"You could do more than stand." I tap his wrist. "I can help you become better. I'm a good teacher. But I won't give you lessons for free."

"Name your price."

"Piroshkies from the bakery outside," I say confidently. My aunt and uncle don't have much money because we're spending all they have on rink fees, my gear, and coaches. "They have the good ones with cabbage and egg. And the sweet ones with cherries. If you bring me a dozen, I'll make you glide like a god."

A muscle jumps in his jaw. "I'll buy you two dozen."

My grin breaks free. "Deal."

We edge back onto the ice. I skate backward, holding his hands, showing him weight over the blades, hips square, chest up, how to roll from inside edge to outside. He complains about everything. The boots are stiff. The ice is too hard. The music is stupid. He still tries what I ask. He wobbles and fights and somehow stays up for a whole length. When he falls again, he sits and stares at the rafters like they personally offended him.

pink right now. "I would hate to see him hurt you. You are a nice girl."

"Thanks for looking out for me." I sigh. "Your papa must be a scary man. No wonder you're rebelling."

"I don't want to be like him," Leo says. "But everyone tells me I'm just like him. That I'll end up doing the same thing he does."

"Crime?"

He shrugs. "Organized crime."

We stand there like that, the two of us fogging up the glass. I point at his feet. "You're locking your knees. Bend a little. It'll help your balance."

"I have balance."

"Not on skates." I push away from the wall, glide backward, and show him my knees. "Soft, like springs. Try."

He tries. He looks like a fridge learning ballet. I bite my lip to kill the laugh that wants out. He glares harder.

"You're tense," I say. "Relax your shoulders."

"You just told me to bend my knees and now you're accusing me of tension."

"Men can multitask." I wink, then gesture. "Again."

He bends more. The wobble lessens. A tiny bit of triumph lights his eyes, then he pushes too hard and spins sideways. I lunge and catch his elbow. The boards thump when we reach them.

He mutters something filthy in Russian. "I'm not graceful."

"No. But you're strong. Learn to control it."

"My father wants me to learn to control other things." He says it like a joke and not a joke. "He expects me to follow him. Take the business one day."

"Do you want that?"

"No."

"Then why are you out here freezing your, um, butt off?"

"Rebelling." He says it flat, like it's boring. "Against my father."

I laugh. I don't mean to. It just jumps out because it's such a weird answer. "You picked the ice rink to rebel?"

"Apparently."

"If you want attention from your parents, steal something. Or punch a boy." I wag a finger like a naughty aunt. "Skating is the opposite of rebellion."

He snorts. "If I did that, my father would be proud."

My mouth tips. "No way. Is your papa a gangster?"

He looks down at his hands. When he looks up, his voice is quiet. "Bratva."

The cold gets a little colder. I've heard that word my whole life, always in whispers or jokes told too loudly by drunk uncles. Bratva is a shadow at the edge of every Russian story. I've never met it face to face. Not like this. Not with a boy whose fingers are warming the rail I touch every day.

"You don't look like a criminal," I say, because my brain is overwhelmed and my mouth likes chaos.

"I'm a criminal's son," he corrects, "so there's a difference."

"I've never met a gangster's son."

His mouth does a weird almost smile that isn't friendly at all. "Now you have. In case you're thinking about reporting me to the police, don't bother." He leans uneasily against the wall, unsteady on his feet. "The police won't help you, and my Papa will break your bones if you make trouble for him. You can forget about your figure skating dream then."

I huff out a white cloud of cold air. "Are you threatening me?"

"I'm protecting you." Leo's gaze meets mine. Being stared at my him makes my cheeks warm. I have no doubt my face is

"You're welcome." I grin, because I can't help it. "First time?"

"What gave it away?"

"The falling on your butt." I tap the glass with my knuckles. "I'm Anya Vasilieva."

He hesitates, then gives me a name like a test. "Leo."

"Nice to meet you, Leo." I shift so he can hold the boards. "I skate here most mornings. I'm training for Russian Junior Nationals."

His eyes flick to mine. They're a stormy gray, cool and a little tired, which is ridiculous on a boy who looks my age. "You're must be good."

"I work hard." It comes out sharper than I mean, so I soften it. I start to ramble, which I don't usually do, unless I'm with an attractive boy who barely speaks. "I started with ballet. Skated at the town pond when I was little, then a tiny rink, then competitions. My coach says I could make Junior Worlds if I nail my jumps and stop psyching myself out. So I'm taking this seriously. I practice every day, even when my legs are about to break. No skipping practices unless I'm dying."

He studies me like I'm a puzzle. I'm used to being watched when I skate, not when I talk. It makes my neck feel warm. There's something rough about him, something that makes me aware of my own femininity. I've never had a crush before. But I could crush on him. He looks like the kind of boy you're supposed to crush on, the kind who wrecks your focus and doesn't even notice. He's strong, silent, handsome, with just the right amount of intrigue.

It really helps that he's quiet and doesn't say dumb things that will turn me off.

"So," I ask, "are you here to be a pro skater, too?"

"No."

World Junior Championships if I keep my head. I pretend I'm not terrified. I'm sixteen. I'm supposed to pretend.

I get here before the other girls because they're my competitors and they try to sabotage me while I'm practicing. Also, I feel self-conscious because I'm not as pretty as them.

I stretch by the boards and look at my reflection in the glass. Bun tight. Laces double-knotted. Nerves under control.

That's when I see him.

He's not a rink boy. Rink boys are wiry and quick, always in hoodies and skate guards with nicked knuckles from doing dumb things for fun. This one is huge. Easily over six feet, broad through the shoulders, muscles fighting his black sweater.

There's ink on his forearms, sharp lines peeking when his sleeves ride up. A tattoo at the rink. Moscow really is not my small town.

He steps onto the ice like it might decide to fight him. His jaw is set, chin high, eyes straight ahead. Dangerous. That's the first word that pops into my head. Dangerous, but also a little lost.

He pushes off. His ankles wobble. He lasts three seconds before gravity wins and he lands on his butt with a sound I feel all the way in my knees.

I don't think. I skate over and crouch. "It's okay. Take my hand. I'll help you up."

Up close he looks even more like trouble. Pretty, in a way I'd never say out loud. His eyes are so beautiful, the color of frozen clouds. His high cheekbones make him look more grown up than his age. His mouth was made for frowning because he looks so sexy doing it.

He glares at my hand like it insulted him, then takes it. He's heavy. I plant my blades and pull. He gets his feet under him, breath coming fast, and I guide him to the wall.

"Thanks," he mutters, like the word costs him money.

When I finish, I drift to the wall. My chest heaves. My legs buzz. He is standing where I left him with a look on his face I've never seen directed at me. Awe. Maybe he's laughing at me inside. He doesn't look like he is.

"You're amazing," he says, voice low. "I've never seen anyone move like that."

Heat climbs my neck. Compliments from the other girls feel like threats. Compliments from coaches are business. This feels different. Like being praised by a fan.

"Thank you," I say, breathless and not just from the program. "If you keep coming, you will improve. I can show you more when I'm finished with practice."

"I'll learn by watching you," he says, stubborn again, but softer at the edges. "Then I'll try."

"Good." I wipe my forehead with the back of my hand. "Don't forget the piroshkies tomorrow."

His mouth does the almost smile again. "I said two dozen."

"Then don't forget two dozen."

I unlatch the gate and head for the locker room. The girls are arriving now, the ones with cat eyes and sharper teeth. They glance at me, then at him, then at me again

In the mirror I see my face, red and sweaty and pleased. I feel a rush of adrenaline. Not from practice, but from the compliment I received from Leo.

I didn't ask him for his last name. Maybe it's better if I don't know.

I wonder if he'll actually come again tomorrow.

I don't have friends here. Not really. I stopped going to school because my hours on the ice and in the gym are precious.

Moscow is loud. It gets quiet at night in a way that makes my chest ache.

Maybe Leo will turn into a boy who looks for me at the

boards. Maybe we'll talk in the mornings about nothing and everything. Maybe I'll show him how to glide without falling, and he'll show me how to make friends with gangsters.

"Piroshkies," I remind myself out loud, and smile like a fool at my reflection.

THREE

Leo

PETROV'S HOUSE sits behind iron fencing and a gate.

The drive curls through clipped hedges to a mansion built to impress auditors and mistresses. White stone. Black windows. A door tall enough for a church. Inside, the air smells like polished wood, old cigar smoke, and cologne.

A maid takes my coat with eyes that never rise above my shoulder. "He is waiting for you in his study. Follow me."

My shoes click across marble into a corridor lined with oil portraits of men.

The study waits at the end, paneled in dark walnut, fire banked low, decanter bright on a tray. Petrov stands behind a desk that is too big for him. His tie is perfect. He is indeed a politician, presenting the image of false perfection, even at home.

"Mr. Antonov," he says, hands spread as if he is about to bless me. "Welcome. I was not sure you would come."

"I said I would." I take the far chair and do not let the leather swallow me. "Where are your wife and son?"

"Out," he says, light and careless. "Shopping. They had some things to buy."

Liar.

I heard a floorboard whisper near the stairs when the maid led me in. I heard a door latch as I crossed the hall. The house is too attentive. He is lying. A thin thread of sound catches my ear now, no more than a breath behind a wall. I keep my face blank.

"St. Petersburg," Petrov begins, pouring himself a drink. "The port is a mess, but I have friends who can deal with matters efficiently. There is a customs issue with a competitor of yours that might be... solvable."

I look at the cut crystal in his hand and think about Aleksandr telling me his papa hits his mama. Words move in the room. I do not care about any of them.

"Excuse me," I say. "Can I use the washroom?"

"Of course. Second door on the right."

I leave the study and walk left. The corridor is as quiet as a church before confession. I pass a gilt mirror, a closed music room, a door that smells faintly of bleach. "Aleksandr," I whisper, barely a sound, as I climb three steps to a half-landing. Another noise answers. Not words. A hurt sound swallowed by a small throat.

The last door is not fully closed. I press my palm to the wood and open it.

The light dizzies me. When it clears, the image before me is even more disorienting.

Anya kneels on a rug beside a narrow bed. The boy lies on his stomach with his shirt pushed high, small fists tight in the blanket. A raw stripe runs across his back, bright and ugly. Anya's hands move in tight circles with a jar of salve.

Her shoulders shake. Tears slip down her face without drama.

The room tilts. I cross it in two strides and drop to a knee so I am level with the boy's eyes. "What happened?" I ask, and my voice is calm in the way avalanches are calm just before they move. "Did Petrov hit you?"

Anya jerks, wild with shock, then covers Aleksandr's shoulders with her body. "Get out," she whispers. The whisper breaks. "Leo, leave. Please."

Aleksandr turns his face toward me. His lashes are wet. When he recognizes me, something like relief lights the wreckage. "You came," he says, small and fierce.

"I said I would." I keep my gaze on him and force my hands to unclench.

My insides are hotter than a furnace. How could Petrov pretend to be a perfect gentleman while his own son is in this state? Clearly, he is a better actor than I gave him credit for. But he's an unfeeling bastard.

I wondered whether Aleksandr had exaggerated his abuse, because he was a child. But it looks like he understated it, if anything.

I drag a hand across the boy's exposed back, feeling his bones and skin. A quiet flutter shakes my stomach. I've seen so much blood, so much agony. Yet, this moves me. A little boy's pain that cannot be forgiven.

Especially now that I know things I didn't know before.

The taste of rage burns like acid down my throat.

"Leo." Anya gathers the boy to her. Her mouth trembles and sets. Unlike her husband, she's a terrible actress. "Why are you here?"

"I came to keep a promise to your son," I say. "And to talk business with your husband." The word tastes foul. "I prefer the first reason."

Anya's back becomes straighter. She protectively curls her hand around Aleksandr, as if I am trying to snatch him away. I couldn't understand her reaction before. I do now. Especially where I'm concerned. "Why would you need to talk to Aleksandr?"

"Aleksandr asked me to make you leave his papa," I say. "He begged me in the parking lot."

Anya stares at the child in her arms. "Is that true?"

Aleksandr nods into her side. "Da, Mama."

Color drains from her face. She pulls him closer, as if proximity could erase the words we have already heard.

"I'm sorry." Anya coughs. Without makeup and in the wan light of the room, she looks older than she should. "Aleksandr is just a child. He doesn't know of the history between us. I don't expect anything from you, Leo. I would prefer if you didn't get involved."

"You want me to walk away after I saw this?" My voice pitches higher, rising like the fury inside me. I point to Aleksandr, to the marks on his back.

Righteousness and the need for justice war in my head. My blood pumps harder than it does during a fight.

"Do not do this," she says, shaking her head. "This is not your concern. I will handle it."

"It is very much my concern." The anger rises, cold and exact. I look at the welt again and then at her. "You should divorce him. You don't look capable of handling this alone."

Her eyes flash. "Leo, you have no right."

I hold her gaze until the room is only the three of us and the sound of both of our hearts. Then I say the thing that has lived like a blade under my tongue since the first moment I saw the boy.

"I have every right, Anya." I enunciate each word with determination. I know the truth now. She tried to hide it, but she couldn't. I knew it the first time I saw Aleksandr. "Aleksandr is my son."

Her gasp is so loud it feels like a bullet punching through the silence.

"No." She swallows, but her eyes give away her guilt. She can't even look at me anymore. She covers Aleksandr's ears, afraid the boy will be confused by my words. Afraid to let him know the truth of his parentage. "That's not true."

"I had a DNA test done. I knew the second I saw your boy that he didn't look like you or his father. But he looked like me. We were together on your wedding night, Anya." I reach into my pocket for my phone and scroll through the messages. I open the document from the lab. "When I stroked his hair at the party, I gathered strands of his hair. I tested them against mine. The result is clear."

I hold up the screen so she can look at the report and read the words.

The phone screen glows between us, its light sharp against the dimness of the room. The words on it are clinical, merciless, undeniable.

Probability of paternity: 99.95%.

My throat tightens. I've read the report a dozen times since the results came in, but watching her see it—watching her freeze—hits me harder than I expected.

Anya closes her eyes as if shutting them can change the truth. Her fingers tremble where they rest on Aleksandr's hair.

"Why didn't you tell me?" My voice is low, but every word cuts.

She opens her eyes, wet and shining. "I never told Petrov, either. He believes Aleksandr is his son."

I rise to my full height, every nerve pulled tight like wire. "You should have told me. I had a right to know."

Her chin lifts, a small act of defiance in the middle of her guilt. "I did what I could do at the time," she says, voice shaking. "I wanted him to have the best childhood possible. I wanted him to have a father who could give him a safe home, an education, and a future that didn't come with blood on it."

My chest burns. "You chose the wrong man, though. Is this the childhood you wanted him to have?" I glance at Aleksandr, still curled against her, his little shoulders quivering from pain and confusion. "A house filled with bruises and silence?"

"Stop." Her voice cracks. She presses Aleksandr's head to her chest, rocking him gently. "Please, Leo. Not now. He doesn't understand. He can't hear this."

The boy blinks up at me, confusion chasing through the fear. I want to tell him everything—that I'm his real father, that I'll protect him, that he'll never have to hide again—but I can't destroy what little calm he has left.

"Go," she begs quietly. "Please. I'll talk to you later. I promise."

For a moment, I can't move. I look at them—the woman who shattered me and the boy who unknowingly carries my blood—and I feel something raw and terrifying bloom in my chest. It's not rage. It's possession. Love, twisted and late.

Anya kisses Aleksandr's temple, whispering something soft in Russian. I crouch down beside them, my voice barely a murmur. "I'll see you again, *synok*."

He nods faintly, eyes heavy with trust he doesn't yet understand.

I rise, sliding my phone back into my pocket. The report might as well be a weapon, and I'm already bleeding from it. My steps are silent as I leave the room, closing the door behind me with a soft click.

Downstairs, Petrov's study still smells like whiskey and arrogance. He looks up when I walk in, unaware that the ground beneath his life has shifted.

"I'll be in touch," I say.

He nods, puzzled, as I stride past him and out of his house.

The cold air hits me like a confession. I stand at the foot of the marble steps, staring at the sky that's turning the color of steel. My pulse hammers. My thoughts are chaos. I've killed men, lost brothers-in-arms, and buried love before, but nothing, nothing has ever felt like this.

I'm a father.

For ten years, I didn't know. For ten years, my son lived under another man's roof, being scared and abused while his real father could have snapped Petrov's neck easily.

Now that I know, there's no going back. I'll have to tell my brothers, eventually. They might not believe it. What I know for sure is that I have to raise Aleksandr. And make sure Anya doesn't suffer anymore. I have to take responsibility for the people I love.

I light a cigarette I don't need, the smoke curling like a vow in the freezing air.

Anya might think she's protecting him. She might think she can shut me out again.

She's wrong.

Because Aleksandr is mine.

And so is she, even if she doesn't know it yet.

FOUR

Anya

TWENTY-SIX YEARS *ago*

HE COMES AGAIN the next day. With two dozen piroshkies, no less.

"You really bought them." My jaw drops. "I can't eat this much. I'll need ten people to finish this."

He shrugs like that's none of his concern. "You should have thought about that before making a deal with me."

I lift the warm paper bag, inhaling the smell of butter and dough. "Well, I can't let them go to waste. You'll have to help me."

"I don't mind," he says, following me to the benches by the glass wall. The rink lights spill over the ice, catching the snow still clinging to his boots.

I take one of the piroshkies and break it open, the

cabbage and egg filling steaming between us. "You know," I tell him, "where I come from, this would feed my whole street."

He glances at me, chewing. "Where are you from?"

"A town called Vyshny Volochyok," I say proudly. "It's small. You can walk from one end to the other in fifteen minutes if you're quick. My papa worked at a textile mill, and my mama taught piano. Every winter, the lake freezes, and that's where I learned to skate. No fancy rinks, just cracked ice and frozen fish underneath."

Leo's lips curve slightly. "Sounds quiet."

"It is." I smile faintly. "Everyone knows everyone. The bakery opens at five. The church bells ring every Sunday whether you want them to or not. I used to complain about it, but now I miss it sometimes."

He leans back on the bench. "I grew up in Moscow. No one knows anyone there, even if they live next door. You hear shouting at night and no one opens the door to help."

"That sounds lonely," I say softly.

He nods once. "My father has money, so we live in a big house. Too big. Marble floors, chandeliers, the whole thing. Still doesn't feel like home."

"You'll buy your own someday," I tease. "A bigger one, once you become a famous figure skater."

He smirks. "You really think I'll make it?"

"Of course." I nudge his shoulder. "You have me as a teacher."

That earns me a small laugh, low and rough. My heart skips a beat. He doesn't laugh often, and when he does, it's like catching sunlight on the ice. Rare and brilliant.

We finish most of the piroshkies together. My stomach aches, but I don't care. I like sitting beside him. I like the sound of his voice when it softens.

"Would you like to hang out outside the rink sometime?" I ask as I tie my skates. "Just, you know... as friends."

He studies me for a moment, unreadable as ever, then nods. "I'd like that."

He is good at keeping his promises, even if he looks like a gangster.

We meet two days later at a public park near the rink. It's one of those gray Moscow afternoons that feels half-asleep. The garden paths are edged with snow, and bare trees shiver against a pale sky. I can't afford cafés or movies, but Leo doesn't seem to care. He walks beside me, hands in his coat pockets, watching the ducks waddle over the frozen pond.

The public park is free, and we can hang out here for as long as we like. It's pretty, too. We don't have places like this in my hometown.

"You like gardens?" I ask, worried he's realized that I'm poor.

"I like watching you like them," he answers simply. His gaze is intently set on me, like I'm something he can't look away from. Like a butterfly. Or a rose.

I bite back a smile. "That's not fair."

"Why?"

"Because you say things that make me blush."

He tilts his head. "You are blushing now."

"Because you called me pretty."

"I didn't."

"Yes, you did."

He grins slightly. "Fine. You're beautiful."

I stare down at my boots, cheeks burning. "I'm your teacher, you know."

"I remember," he says, his voice dropping, teasing. "Doesn't change anything."

We walk in silence for a while, the kind of silence that feels comfortable, not awkward.

He stops near the gate and looks at me. "I've been thinking," he says. "Figure skating might not be for me. I don't have the patience for it. Or the grace."

I laugh softly. "You don't say."

"Maybe I'll go into business instead."

"You don't look like a businessman," I tell him honestly.

"I don't look like a figure skater either."

"Touché." I smile. "Maybe you'll surprise everyone."

"Maybe." His eyes catch mine for a beat too long, and I feel it. Something unspoken, something dangerous and sweet at the same time.

"I'll be gone next weekend," I say quickly, breaking the spell. A strange ache fills my chest, and it feels like I'm underwater. I realize I'll miss Leo. I haven't known him for long, but he seems to have carved a space for himself in my heart. My chest aches sometimes at night when I need someone to talk to but he isn't there. "Competition in St. Petersburg."

He nods. "Then I'll wish you luck now. You'll win."

"Maybe," I whisper. "If I'm lucky."

We keep walking, talking about nothing and everything—music, food, stupid movies we've never seen. It's easy. Easier than it's ever been with anyone.

For the first time in years, I feel like I have a friend.

Maybe more than that.

When he walks me back to the bus stop, the city feels warmer somehow.

And for the first time since I came to Moscow, I don't feel quite so alone.

FIVE

Leo

ALEKSEI CAN TELL I'm not the same. My younger brother has always been perceptive. It's probably because we're only a few years apart. Aleksei and Mikhail are almost like real siblings to me.

Dmitry and Nikolai, my two youngest brothers, were toddlers when our parents were killed in a car crash engineered by their enemies. I had to raise them like a father, and I fear I may not have been such a good father because Nikolai got a girl pregnant in high school, and Dmitry, while academically brilliant, seems to be as emotionally stifled as I am.

I sigh while looking at the clouds from Aleksei's mansion. I feel old now. I raised my brothers, created an empire with them, and now that the next generation is here, it makes me feel like a dinosaur.

"Lena's not at home, is she?" I ask.

"She's out with Zorina. I told her not to move around too much while she's pregnant, but she never listens."

Aleksei's husbandly manner makes me wince. He got married to his much younger American wife two years ago. He got her pregnant when she was a part of the secret society that we control at one of the most prestigious colleges in the United States. Now his wife's pregnant with their second child. Lena hates me, though. I didn't like her, either, and even now, while I know she has made Aleksei very happy, I wouldn't have picked her.

I should leave before she comes back home, or she might kill me. Or at least give me a very nasty, stinky eye. She has made peace with seeing me around, but even now, we're uneasy around each other. The scars from the past are impossible to forget, even among family.

But I like staying with family even if it's complicated. And Lena bakes good cookies. Right now, I don't think I could take the silence and emptiness of a hotel. Not while I'm grappling with the biggest realization in the world.

"You never contemplate. Something big must have happened," Aleksei comments.

I don't reply. I can't confess the extent of my problems right now. He will try to help me. I will be needing his help in the future, but not right now. I am the pakhan, the patriarch of this family. That means I can't lean on anyone, even though they can all lean on me. I've always felt the weight of the title. I didn't even want it, but I don't regret being what I am. It's what allowed me to give my brothers a home, a materially comfortable life, and now that I see them building families and fulfilling their dreams, my decades of sacrifices seem worth it.

Except a small, niggling part of me wishes I'd known about my own biological son earlier.

"Daddy!" I'm saved from answering when my niece

Anechka runs into the room. She's adorable, and even my cold heart softens when she's close to me. She's growing so much every day, and even I like watching her learn and do new things. I'm just her uncle.

"Uncle Leo." She claws at my knee, and I pick her up, placing her on my lap where she bounces happily. I don't kiss her head. I'm not that affectionate. I've been in control for too long to give affection easily. When Anechka tries to kiss my cheek, I push her away.

I stare at Aleksei while he watches with worry, anxious that I'll scar his daughter with my authoritative, patriarchal ways.

A sudden realization hits me: I kissed Aleksandr's head without a second thought. Back in Moscow, I did it on instinct. I couldn't believe it myself.

Something prickles in my chest when I realize I never saw Aleksandr grow up. And now I will never know what that feels like.

"How does it feel to be a father?" I ask, instead.

Aleksei raises his eyebrow. "Why do you want to know? You said it yourself that you don't want to get married or have kids."

"Forget I asked, then."

"You are being very strange today. Did something happen?"

"The business is hard," I say, vaguely. "Things happen every day."

"If something was really bad, Dmitry would be fretting over it. He seems preoccupied these days. He has been recruiting new people into the society."

"Yeah, he told me about his plan. It's a good idea. Let's see if he can execute it."

"He has brains, so he probably can," Aleksei answers.

"Watch over him," I say. "He's still young. Help him if he needs it."

"That goes without saying. We're brothers, aren't we?" Aleksei takes Anechka from my lap, and she fusses around, pulling her father's beard.

Aleksei is the enforcer of the Antonov bratva. He's a big, muscular, tattooed man who looks menacing. But he's a teddy bear for his wife and daughter. How can someone be so different around different people? Is it because he doesn't feel like he has to play a role that requires attention and focus 24/7?

"I'm going back to Moscow tonight," I tell him. "I won't be sleeping over."

"Why?" Aleksei quirks a brow. "You have something urgent? You can stay here for the night."

"I'm dealing with a new politician. He seems eager to help us with the St. Petersburg port."

This makes Aleksei's jaw tighten. He's our enforcer. He likes finding out about people, knowing if they could be dangerous, if they are connected to our enemies and can threaten our lives, even though that's part of Dmitry's job. "Who?"

"Petrov. He's not that important."

"If he wasn't important, you wouldn't be interested in him."

"Maybe I'm interested in him for other reasons."

Aleksei rocks Anechka in his arms. His big, muscular arms are so huge, and she's tiny. He hesitates, opening his mouth, then closing it. "Leo, are you…" He trails off, shaking his head.

"What?" I come to my feet.

"Never mind. It's ridiculous."

"What is?"

"Leo, are you gay? Is that why you don't want to marry? I know we grew up in the Soviet Union, and things were hard for homosexuals, but we're in America now. Dmitry and Nikolai would accept you. Mikhail is pretty Americanized, too. You don't have to worry about us."

I roll my eyes. This is what I get for telling my brother I'm interested in Petrov *'for other reasons'*.

"No, I'm not homosexual. I wouldn't judge any of our brothers for being so, so I'm glad we're on the same page. That's why I brought you all to America. I wanted you to live a life better than mine."

"And yet, you were against me marrying an American girl?"

"She was too young," I protest. "And she was distracting you. She didn't seem trustworthy."

"That's my wife you are talking about."

I fold my arms over my chest. "Maybe I should leave for Moscow now."

"Yeah, be gone before Lena comes back home and spots you." Aleksei jokes. "She still hasn't forgiven you for almost getting her killed two years ago. She might poison your dinner as revenge."

Two years ago, I thought I was looking out for Dmitry. I wanted to make sure she was loyal. It's always different with women who aren't Russian, who haven't been raised in Bratva families. They're not used to the way the bratva functions, or the rules they'll have to abide by. They think they can get a divorce and leave if things get scary, but the bratva is like a blood family—these ties bind forever.

Which is why I understand why Anya didn't want anyone to know that Aleksandr was my son. I'm a very wanted man in Russia. My son would constantly be in danger. The moment word gets out about me being Aleksandr's father, his life will never be safe.

Even the shadows will not hide him.

THE APARTMENT IS SMALL, too modest for her. A quiet building tucked behind an old bookstore, the kind of place that doesn't draw attention. I like it. It feels safer than her husband's mansion ever could.

Anya opens the door herself, wrapped in a cream wool coat and that same fragile composure she always wears when she sees me. Her lips part, then tighten again.

"You came," she says softly.

"Did I ever break my promises to you?"

"Once," she reminds me. "You didn't come to see me skate at the World Figure Skating Championships final."

"My parents died that day," I say.

She nods softly. "I'm sorry. I shouldn't have reminded you of something you wanted to forget."

She steps aside, and I follow her into a narrow sitting room. A single lamp glows near the window, its light glinting off the polished samovar on the side table. The air smells like mint tea.

"Let me," I murmur, reaching for her coat. She hesitates but lets me help. My fingers brush the silk lining as I slide it from her shoulders. Her skin is warm beneath the fabric, the curve of her neck pale in the lamplight.

For a second, I forget everything—Petrov, the bratva, the years between us. I lower my head and kiss her shoulder, slow and reverent.

She gasps, spinning around to face me. "Leo, don't."

"Old habits," I say, voice low.

"Bad ones."

"I'm a bad man, Anya. You know that already." I gesture to the chair near the window. "Sit."

She crosses the room and sits, posture perfect as if she's back on the ice, waiting for the music to start.

"Where's Aleksandr?" I ask.

"At my aunt's." Her hands twist in her lap. "I didn't want

him to hear... any of this. He's still young. If he finds out the truth now, he'll be confused. Maybe even angry."

"He doesn't seem to like Petrov much," I say carefully.

"He doesn't," she admits. "But I'm his mother, Leo. I've raised him. I know what's best for him. I can't tell him yet. Not until he's older and he can understand the world that you come from. He might wonder how I had your kid while I was married to Petrov. And he might tell other people that you're his dad, not knowing the consequences. That will make things hard for the both of us."

I nod slowly. She's right in one sense. If word ever got out that Aleksandr is mine, the boy would never be safe. My enemies would use him as leverage. The Sokolov Syndicate would use him as bait.

I have lived in the underworld long enough to know that it isn't a good place. That's why I never wanted to have kids in the first place.

"You want to stay married to that man?"

Her gaze flicks up, startled. "I want Aleksandr safe."

"I can make you divorce him, Anya," I say quietly. "Make him divorce you, whether you wanted to or not."

Her brows knit. "How?"

"I could reduce Petrov's life to hell. I could strip him of everything he owns, drive him into debt so deep he'd beg for mercy. Then I'd offer him a way out. I'd demand that he divorce you in exchange for his freedom from the bratva's grip. What do you think he'll do in that situation?"

She stares at me, horror and disbelief twisting together. "You think like a gangster."

"I *am* a gangster, *milaya*."

She shakes her head. "You used to say you didn't want to be one."

"I realized this is the only thing I'm good at."

Her voice softens, almost a whisper. "Isn't that what your father used to tell you?"

The words hit harder than any bullet. I look away, jaw tight. "Maybe."

She studies me for a moment, then asks, "Do you think I hate you for what you are?"

I meet her eyes. "Do you?"

"No," she says quietly. "I never hated you. But now that I've seen what my husband really is—a man who destroys people with laws instead of bullets—I don't think there are any good men left."

I almost smile. "Cynicism doesn't suit you, *malishka*. You used to believe the world could be fixed with a perfect performance."

"That was a long time ago."

"So, do you want to divorce him," I ask, tapping my finger against the armrest, "or should I make you do it?"

The air between us thickens. Her pulse beats visibly in her throat. Then, without a word, she stands.

"Anya?"

She reaches for the zipper of her dress. The sound rips through the silence. I take a step forward, but she doesn't stop. The fabric slides from her shoulders, pooling at her feet.

"What are you doing?" My voice drops, rough.

I haven't seen her naked in a decade. As her dress falls away, revealing her body. The creamy swells of her ass cheeks peek through her lace panties, igniting a flame in my groin. My eyes trace her wide hips that bore a child, her sexy, creamy thighs. All I can fixate on is how much more beautiful she has become.

And how much more tragic. Beneath the dress, her skin is a canvas of old pain—bruises fading to yellow, new ones still dark and angry. She turns around. Thin scars lace across her ribs.

Rage sears through me. "How long has this been happening?"

She hugs her arms around herself, trembling. "Years." Her voice breaks. "I endured it, Leo. I'll keep enduring it if I have to. As long as Aleksandr stays safe."

"Safe?" I snarl. "Your son doesn't want this. He wants you free. He told me himself."

She shakes her head, tears spilling freely now. "There's no freedom for me. Not really. If I divorce him, I'll get nothing but scraps of money. I'll always have to look over my shoulder, wondering if someone finds out the truth about Aleksandr—that he's yours—and decides to punish me for it. Petrov's position and power could protect Aleksandr, that's why I chose to stay."

"Then why?" I yell at her, my temper escaping its leash. "Why did you have him, if you knew what you were walking into? You must have suspected he was mine."

Anya closes her eyes, her shoulders shaking. "Because he was yours," she says. "And I loved you."

The world stills. I can't breathe.

Her confession lands like a blade to the chest—sharp, clean, and final.

I know Anya loved me. And yet, why does her confession sting so much? She doomed herself to a life of constant threat and fear by giving birth to my son.

"If you loved me, then face the consequences of loving me." The restlessness thundering through my insides crackles. I feel electricity pressing against my skin, fighting to get out.

My fingers make a brutal sound when I ball them into fists. The crack of bones reverberates through the air.

Anya's lips part. Here, before me, naked and scarred, she looks more vulnerable and beautiful than she ever did. The urge to smooth my hands over the markings on her skin, the marks she let Petrov carve because she was trying to protect our love in a twisted way, is unbearable.

My feet pause an inch away from her bare toes. I'm so close to her, I could lean over and push her against the wall. I can feel her body heat. Her tits pressing against my chest. My cock tightens. A rush of blood makes my groin feel painful.

I need to fuck her. But before that, I need to make her feel safe.

"Let me touch you." I'm not the kind of man who asks for permission for anything. I take by force. "You deserve some comfort, Anya. You've been living in that hell for too long. You can't hold out forever alone. It will kill you. He hit Aleksandr the other day. It's already out of your control. You must know that, too."

I reach over and unclasp her bra. The sound is sharp and perfect.

When the fabric falls away, Anya's round, beautiful breasts spill free.

"Christ," I mutter under my breath, awed by the sight of them. "You really have changed since the last time I saw you naked."

Her breasts are much bigger than before, plump and soft like big melons. I feel their weight, holding them in my palms.

"So perfect," I mutter. "Motherhood has made you utterly ravishing."

I scoop up the fat globes of her tits, sinking my fingers into their softness. The ice in my veins melts the moment the warmth from her skin seeps through my fingertips. Fire replaces the coldness. An inferno roars in my blood vessels. Touching her is intoxicating. I crush her breasts, teasing her nipples, listening to her pleasure-soaked cries as she gives up her resistance.

My stomach clenches in response. The painful brush of my cock's sensitive head against my boxers sets my blood ablaze.

Anya's eyes are filled with the blackness of her pupils. She breaths raggedly, inching backward, away from me, until her back hits the wall.

I won't let her get away. Not this time. Not when she needs this as much as I do. She needs a release from the constant stress and anxiety of keeping up a charade.

I tease her plump bottom lip with my thumb, tracing its fullness. She moans, arching her back, pressing her breasts to me. The peaks are diamond-hard, needy little points begging for my mouth.

"Leo...I...."

"What?" I grind my teeth, anger spiking the volume of my words. "Don't tell me you want to be faithful to that bastard. He doesn't deserve any loyalty from you."

"Leo, if we do this...I won't be able to live in that darkness anymore. Do you know how many times I wanted take Aleksandr and run away from Petrov's house because he never made my body feel like you did? My pussy craved you on nights when I was lonely. My heart longed for your voice."

"Then why didn't you leave?" I raise an eyebrow. "He wouldn't have missed you."

"I thought I should let you go. I was the one who rejected your proposal. I broke your heart. I was scared to be involved with the bratva. I held myself back because I knew I didn't deserve your love or your protection."

I cup her face roughly. "You should have come to me. I would have forgiven you."

"I didn't deserve your forgiveness. Also, I didn't know if you had another woman. As the years passed, I wondered if you had gotten married to someone else. An arranged marriage for your organization's benefit. I had no way to know," she replies. "Sometimes...I imagined it. You fucking another woman the way you fucked me. Another woman carrying your child, her belly swollen like mine."

I tighten my fingers on her jaw. "And what did that make you feel?"

"Despair," she replies, her eyes misty.

"Can you imagine how I felt, knowing you were fucking another man and I couldn't do anything about it?"

"I'm sorry."

"You should be." I slide my hands down the slope of her slim, elegant neck. "And I'll make you pay for making me feel that way, Anya. Tonight, I'm going to sink my cock into you and remind you of all the reasons you should leave your husband for me."

She jerks when I slide a hand behind her. I slap the perfectly rounded globe of her ass cheek. The cry she releases is sweet music to my dick. My cock is swollen, and my balls are clenching from the denial.

"Turn around. I want to watch your ass bounce when I fuck you."

Anya doesn't protest this time. She doesn't even ask me to kiss her, to make this romantic or tender, because I plan to give her neither. Not until she begs for me. Not until she surrenders to me and agrees to be mine for life.

I used to give her everything freely, but betrayal has taught me cruelty.

I roughly flip her around, pressing her breasts against the wall. She gasps, her palms flat against the cold surface, her back arching slightly as if offering herself to me. I can see the curve of her spine, the smooth skin marred by faint bruises, and it fuels my anger and desire. I want to replace every mark on her body with my own, claim her, remind her who she belongs to.

I hook my fingers into the waistband of her panties and tear them away in one swift motion. The sound of the fabric ripping is satisfying, as is the sharp intake of her breath. I kick her legs apart, spreading her wide for me. She's exposed, vulnerable, her pussy glistening with wetness that tells me she's as aroused as she is afraid.

I thrust my fingers between her legs, feeling the slick warmth of her cunt. She's soaking wet, her folds swollen and needy. I stroke her gently at first, teasing her, listening to the soft whimpers that escape her lips. My fingers glide through her wetness, circling her clit, feeling it throb under my touch.

"You're dripping, malishka," I murmur, my voice a low growl in her ear. "Is this for me, or do you get this wet for him too?"

She shakes her head vigorously. "Only you, Leo. Always only you."

I reward her with a harsh laugh, my fingers moving faster, spreading her wetness up to her clit and down to her tight little hole. I press one finger inside her, feeling her pussy grip me tightly, desperate for more.

"Look at you, so eager," I taunt, adding a second finger, pumping them in and out of her with brutal force. "You're a mess, Anya. A hot, wet mess. You should see how your cunt is clenching around my fingers, like it wants to suck them in deeper."

She moans, her hips moving in sync with my thrusts. I add a third finger, stretching her, preparing her for my cock. My thumb finds her clit, rubbing it in tight circles, making her cry out.

"That's it, malishka," I coo, my voice dripping with cruelty. "Moan for me. Let me hear how much you love being fucked by my fingers. Is this what you wanted all those nights you spent alone in his bed? Did you dream of me touching you like this?"

She nods, her breath coming in short gasps. "Yes, so many times. Sometimes my pussy hurt from clenching for you."

I can feel her getting closer, her body tensing, her pussy dripping. I curl my fingers inside her, hitting that spot that makes her scream. She comes hard, her body convulsing, her pussy clamping down on my fingers, soaking them with her release.

I don't give her time to recover. I spin her around, lift her leg, and thrust into her, sheathing my cock in her still-spasming pussy. She cries out, her nails digging into my shoulders, her eyes wide with shock and pleasure.

"Leo!" she screams, her voice hoarse.

I grunt, my hips moving, my cock pounding into her. I'm not gentle. I can't be. Not with the rage and desire coursing through me. I want to punish her, remind her who she belongs to, who can make her feel like this.

"You're mine, Anya," I growl, my hips slapping against hers, my cock filling her completely. "You've always been mine. You should have never left me. You should have never kept my son from me."

She wraps her arms around my neck, her body taking my punishment, her pussy welcoming each brutal thrust. "I'm sorry," she sobs. "I'm so sorry, Leo."

I can feel her tears on my neck, her body shaking, her pussy milking my cock. The emotion and physical intensity of the moment are overwhelming. It's raw, primal, a claiming and a surrender all at once.

I reach between us, finding her clit, rubbing it as I fuck her. I want her to come again. I want to feel her pussy squeeze my cock, feel her orgasm coat me. I want to breed her, mark her, make her mine again.

"Come for me, Anya," I demand, my voice harsh. "Give me what I deserve."

She does, her body convulsing, her pussy gripping my cock so tightly it triggers my own release. I come with a roar, my cock pulsing, filling her with my seed. I breed her roughly, making sure she takes every drop, every last piece of me.

We stay like that for a moment, our bodies joined, our breaths syncing. I can feel her heartbeat against my chest, can feel the flutter of her pussy as it milks the last of my release. I pull back slightly, looking into her eyes, seeing the mix of fear, pleasure, and possession in them.

"You can't run away from me again, Anya," I say again, my voice softer this time but no less firm. "It's time you face the truth. There's no way to protect Aleksandr except taking my offer. I'm the only one who can protect you both. Not your husband. He can't protect you from me now that I want you. So go back to his pathetic house for now. But don't forget that you can't avoid me forever."

SIX

Anya

TWENTY-FOUR YEARS AGO...

MOSCOW WINTERS ARE THE WORST.

My toes are like little icicles by the time I arrive at the street where my uncle lives. It's quiet and empty, lined by multistoried buildings from the Soviet era. It's not as elegant as some of the newer neighborhoods, but it carries a familiar charm. It's home.

Ever since my figure skating career took off, my parents sent me to Moscow to live with my uncle and aunt. They don't have any children, and they were happy to support my promising career.

Tonight, my heart is still racing, not from the cold, but from the competition. From the scores. From my name announced over loudspeakers and applause that felt too big to belong to me.

I won. It was even on TV. I landed all my jumps except one, and got the best score of my career. I couldn't believe it. At first, I thought I was dreaming. But when they handed me the trophy and put the gold medal around my neck, it all started to feel more real.

My coach was ecstatic. He drove me back home, promising that I could take a rest day tomorrow.

My heart is still soaring. I might never come down from the high of winning the national championships. This means I can go skate at the world championships. I will be travelling abroad. I'm eighteen now, so I guess I'm a big girl.

I mean, I even have a boyfriend.

Leo Antonov's head turns toward me. He's so huge, completely out of place on the street. He looks like a thug, with his tattoos and the small bruises on his face.

But he's still handsome. And only I know that beneath all that roughness and darkness, he's a sweet man who holds me when I cry after losing competitions.

He doesn't ask anything of me. He doesn't skate anymore, but he still comes to watch me practice sometimes at the rink. We go on long walks afterward. For a year, that's all we did. We became good friends. I know his favorite shows and I know he still doesn't have a dream.

We've been dating for months now, ever since the day he fell on the ice and took me down with him a year ago, our skates tangling, our laughter dissolving into something breathless and charged. He kissed me then, wild and impulsive, like he didn't know how to hold anything back. I should have stopped it. I knew that. His father was a gangster. Nothing about his life was safe or simple.

But I didn't stop him.

Leo is a good boyfriend. Better than I ever imagined having. He buys me piroshkies when I'm exhausted, waits outside the rink when I'm too tired to speak, and cheers for me when I doubt myself. I even introduced him to my aunt and uncle, telling them his parents run a business. They like him. Everyone does.

His face breaks into a grin when he sees me. "I saw you on TV," he says, pushing off the railing and crossing the distance in two strides. "You were incredible. Congratulations on winning gold. My girlfriend is the best."

Before I can answer, he pulls me into his arms. He smells like cold air and leather and something unmistakably him. Then he kisses me, quick and warm, right there on the sidewalk.

I laugh, cheeks burning. "Leo, stop. The neighbors will see."

"So?" he murmurs, clearly unbothered. "They should get used to it."

I roll my eyes, but I'm smiling. "You're impossible."

"I'm generous," he counters. "I'm also planning to give you a proper gift later. After your aunt and uncle are asleep."

My pulse stutters. I know what he means. Or maybe I only think I do. The thought makes my stomach flutter with nerves and anticipation. Is tonight the night?

We've been talking about having sex. The chemistry between us is insane. Sometimes, when we're close, I feel like the place between my legs is going to explode. A few weeks ago, he touched my breasts and I rubbed his hard cock. That's when I knew we had to do it. There was no going back. We're going to get sick if we don't fuck each other. Sometimes, the ache between my legs gets unbearable, and only imagining his weight pressing against my private parts is enough to cool me down.

I should probably wait for marriage, but Leo is wild and untamed. When I'm with him, I want to be that way, too. He releases me from the burdens of routines, the pressure of winning, and the uncertainty of my future. I can let loose, be just Anya Vasilieva, not the golden girl whose parents' hopes are riding on me.

"I remembered you," I tell him softly. I reach into my coat and close my fingers around the little charm he gave me weeks ago. "I carried this with me the whole time."

His expression changes, something tender breaking through the bravado. "I've never wanted anyone to win the way I wanted you to."

"No one ever has," I admit. "I bet the other girls at the rink will be really jealous. Then again, they don't have a boyfriend who buys them lucky charms."

He cups my face with one gloved hand. "Your win is mine, too. I get to live my dream through you. Watching you skate makes me believe things can be different."

I notice it then, a thin cut near his hairline, already healing. My fingers lift without thinking, tracing it gently. "What happened?" I whisper. "Did your father make you do something?"

His jaw tightens. "It's nothing."

But I know better. He quit the rink after his father threatened to shut it down. Since then, every day feels like borrowed time. I'm terrified he's slipping away from me, being pulled deeper into a world I can't follow, becoming someone harder and colder than the boy who once dreamed beside me on the ice.

I lace my fingers through his. "Come on," I say, forcing brightness into my voice. "My aunt cooked enough food to feed an army."

He squeezes my hand, and together we climb the stairs, our

steps light and hopeful, as if the night hasn't already begun to ask for more than we're ready to give.

Leo is quiet throughout dinner. He smiles at the right moments, thanks my aunt for the food, compliments my uncle's stories, but it all feels practiced. His eyes keep drifting away, like he's somewhere else entirely. He's more withdrawn than usual.

Something definitely happened. He came to celebrate my win, but I don't want him to pretend to be happy if he isn't.

My aunt and uncle let him stay over because it's late. He sleeps in the guest bedroom.

I wait until the apartment settles into sleep, until the pipes stop knocking and my aunt's soft snores float through the thin walls. Then I pad barefoot across the hallway and knock once, lightly.

"Leo," I whisper.

There's a sound inside. A sharp movement. Then something heavy hits the floor.

I open the door.

He's standing by the bed, shoulders tense, eyes wide. On the rug between us lies a black shape that does not belong in my uncle's house.

I stare at it. "Is that a gun?"

He exhales slowly, like he's been holding his breath all evening. "Yes, malishka, it's exactly what it looks like."

My heart stutters. I step closer and crouch, careful, and pick it up the way I've seen on television, by the grip, finger nowhere near the trigger. It's heavier than I expect. Real.

I hand it back to him. "What are you going to do with it?"

He takes it and sets it on the bedside table, then looks at me in a way that makes my chest ache. He doesn't answer. He just stands there, silent and shaking, and I know.

I step into him and wrap my arms around his waist.

He breaks. His arms come around me hard, crushing me to his chest. His breath stutters against my hair. "My father gave it to me today," he says hoarsely. "He said it's time I learned how to kill. He said I need to take over. I'm supposed to carry this everywhere now, in case someone tries to shoot me. I'm a full-fledged gangster now."

My stomach turns cold. "Leo..."

"I shouldn't be telling you this," he says quickly. "I shouldn't ruin this for you. You won today. You were perfect. I should have kept my mouth shut. Can you forget what I said?"

"I want to hear more," I urge him. "I want to know what's troubling you. And by the way, whatever you said doesn't ruin my victory at all. This and that are separate matters."

He pulls back, scrubbing a hand over his face. He looks so vulnerable. I have seen him look this way multiple times, and every time, it came with bad news. The first time, his dad hit him and locked him in a dark room for two whole days. He came back to the rink looking like a corpse. The other times, he had gotten major injuries during fights or 'work' as he called it.

Leo swallows, looking at me with guilt stamped across his features. "I shot a man with that gun. I didn't kill him. But there was blood." He laughs, sharp and broken. "I'm sorry. I'm so sorry."

I step back into him and hold him tighter, my hands sliding up into his hair. "You never have to hide with me," I whisper. "Never. I want to be here for you when it's hard. The way you're always here for me."

He stiffens. "You shouldn't be. You should break up with me. You don't know what kind of monster I am."

I pull back just enough to look at him. "You're *my* monster, Leo Antonov. And I'll love you till the day I die."

His brow furrows. "That's not funny."

"I'm not joking." My voice is steady, even as my heart races.

"Knowing a monster who would kill for me could be useful someday. You know, if I end up making enemies."

He huffs a weak laugh. "You're impossible. Always looking for the silver lining. Is there anything you can't put a positive spin on?"

He leans down and presses his forehead to mine. "You know, that's why I fell in love with you."

My breath catches.

"When I'm with you," he continues, quieter now, "I can forget who I am. I can forget what I am. Because you're the light that erases my shadows."

"You're not a bad person," I say.

"You don't know that." His voice drops. "When I shot that man today... I felt it. The adrenaline. The rush. I wanted more. Maybe I'm more like my father than I thought. I like winning. I like blood when it means I've won. I don't think I'd have cared if he died."

The words should terrify me. Instead, something settles into place.

"I always knew you were wild," I say softly. "Dangerous. Dark. Something about your brokenness calls out to me. I don't think you're unlovable. Just intense."

He looks at me like I've struck him.

"I still want you," I tell him. "Even if everything goes wrong. Even if you disappear one day. You're the only person I've ever loved. What we have matters to me."

His hands slide to my waist, grounding himself. He leans his forehead against mine again, breathing me in.

"I don't deserve you," he murmurs.

"Maybe," I say gently. "But I'm here anyway."

He tackles me onto the bed, his weight pressing me into the mattress. My breath catches as he leans over me, his face so close I can see the storm in his gray eyes. The heat radiating from his body makes the space between my legs clench with anticipation.

"Really?" His voice is rough, almost desperate. "Will you love me even if fuck you right here tonight? Will you let me?"

My heart pounds so hard I'm sure he can hear it. "Would that make you feel better?"

"No," he admits, his thumb tracing my bottom lip. "But it will make me forget. For a little while, I can pretend I'm someone worth having."

I reach up and cup his face. "Then have me. I would never give my first time to anyone but you."

Something breaks in his expression—restraint, maybe, or the last thread of his control. "You're crazy," he breathes. "But I'm a monster, so I don't care. I'll take advantage of you. I'll leave you too sore to walk."

"I know," I whisper.

He captures my mouth in a kiss that steals my breath, his tongue sliding against mine with hunger and need. His hands move to my nightgown, and I hear the fabric tear as he pulls it apart. Cool air hits my skin, followed immediately by the heat of his palms.

"You're so beautiful," he murmurs against my throat, trailing kisses down to my collarbone. "So fucking perfect."

I gasp as his mouth finds my breast, his tongue circling my nipple before he takes it between his lips. The sensation shoots straight to my core, making me arch against him. His hand cups my other breast, kneading gently, his thumb brushing over the sensitive peak.

"Leo," I breathe, my fingers threading through his hair.

He moves lower, kissing a path down my stomach. His hands slide to my thighs, spreading them apart. I should feel embarrassed, exposed like this, but the way he looks at me—like

I'm something precious and profane all at once—makes shame impossible.

"So soft," he says, his lips brushing the inside of my thigh. "I want to taste every inch of you."

He kisses higher, closer to where I'm aching for him. When his mouth finally finds me there, I cry out, my hips lifting off the bed. His tongue explores me with deliberate strokes, learning what makes me gasp, what makes me moan.

"That's it, malishka," he encourages, his voice vibrating against my sensitive flesh. "Let me hear you."

The pleasure builds until I'm trembling, my hands fisting in the sheets. Just when I think I can't take anymore, he pulls back, moving up my body. I whimper at the loss.

"Shh," he soothes, kissing my lips so I can taste myself on his tongue. "I've got you."

He positions himself between my thighs. I feel the hard length of him pressing against my entrance. Our eyes meet.

"This might hurt," he warns, his voice strained with the effort of holding back.

"I trust you," I tell him.

He pushes forward slowly, and I feel the stretch, the burn as my body adjusts to accommodate him. I gasp, my nails digging into his shoulders.

"Breathe," he instructs, holding still despite the tension in his muscles. "Just breathe, solnyshka."

I do, forcing air into my lungs. The initial pain begins to fade, replaced by a fullness that feels overwhelming and right all at once.

"More," I whisper.

He moves deeper, inch by inch, kissing my face, my neck, my shoulders—gentle touches that contrast with the claiming of my body. When he's fully seated inside me, we both go still, adjusting to the connection.

"You okay?" he asks, his forehead pressed to mine.

"Yes," I manage. "Move. Please."

He does, pulling back before sliding home again. The friction is exquisite. Each thrust builds the pleasure higher, erasing everything but the feel of him inside me, the scent of our skin, the sound of our breathing.

"Mine," he growls against my ear. "You're mine, Anya. Say it."

"Yours," I gasp. "Always yours."

His pace increases, becoming rougher, more primal. The bed frame creaks beneath us. My body rises to meet his thrusts, chasing something I don't fully understand but desperately need.

"That's my girl," he praises. "Take me. Take all of me."

The pressure coils tighter in my core until it snaps. An inferno rages through my body, pumping through my veins like the most exquisite drug. I reach my peak, and then he pushes me even higher by ramming his cock into my aching pussy. Waves of pleasure submerge me, making my mind go blank. He follows moments later, burying himself deep as he finds his own release. I feel him release cum into my channel. I take every bit of it, feeling a forbidden delight as it trickles out of my pussy, smearing onto my thighs.

"I love you," he whispers into my hair. "I don't deserve you, but I love you."

I press a kiss over his heart. "I love you, too."

Outside, snow begins to fall, blanketing Moscow in white. But here, in this small room, we create our own warmth, our own world where the darkness can't quite reach.

For tonight, at least, we're just Leo and Anya—two people in love, holding each other against everything that wants to tear us apart.

SEVEN

Leo

I STILL SEE her scars in my dreams. I can't forget them. I can't forget the pain she showed me. And I know I need to do something to get her out of Petrov's clutches fast.

But every good plan requires time and patience. Especially delicate ones. Getting her to divorce him won't be hard. If she initiates, I don't think he'll resist. I even have plans to introduce him to a better woman, one who will help his political career. He'll pick her over Anya any second. That's the kind of opportunistic man he is.

I take the burner phone from the drawer and dial the number I memorized the night I gave it to her. It rings twice.

"Leo?" Her voice is cautious, already braced for bad news.

"I spoke to my lawyer," I say. "I wanted you to hear it from me first. He'll call you soon and get the divorce moving. Quietly."

She exhales. I can hear it. "That fast?"

"He's good."

"And if Petrov causes trouble?"

"He won't," I say. "But if he does, I'll deal with it."

There's a pause. Then, softer, "He might try for custody."

"He won't get it."

"You're sure?"

"My lawyer will make sure you do," I say evenly. "Petrov wouldn't want stories about abusing his wife or a child touching daylight. His image matters more than anything. He'll do what he's told."

A small sound escapes her, something close to a laugh. "Is your lawyer as good with threats as you are?"

"Better," I reply. "It's his job."

She goes quiet again. Then, "Thank you."

I lean back in the chair and close my eyes. "You don't have to thank me."

"I do," she insists. "You're sticking your neck out for me."

"For my family," I correct.

Her voice tightens. "Leo, I've been thinking. Aleksandr and I will move to my parents' town for a while. It's safer. Quieter. I don't want to be a burden to you anymore."

"You're not a burden."

"And since no one knows you're his father, it's for the best," she continues, pushing on. "If we start dating. If we get married. He becomes a target. I won't risk that. It's better if we stay away from each other."

I open my eyes. The city outside my window looks flat and distant. "You want to pretend I had nothing to do with your divorce."

"Yes," she says. "Petrov will never find out anyway."

She's right. I know she is. Wanting her, claiming her publicly, would paint a target on her back. On my son's. I've already let her go too many times for the sake of logic and fear.

"This time," I say slowly, "I don't want to be reasonable."

"Leo."

"I'm selfish," I admit. "I'm too old to be selfless now."

"You're not listening."

"I am." I soften my voice. "Go to your parents' house if you want. Or to your aunt's. Do what you need to do. But don't lie to yourself. Your body needs me even if you don't."

Silence hums between us.

"I won't pressure you," I continue. "I could force my way into your life. You know that. But I can't stay unless you let me. This time, I want you to choose. I want you to choose once and forever."

Her breath shudders. "Thank you. For understanding."

"I don't understand," I say. "I accept."

She hesitates. "I'll repay you. Any way I can."

"I don't want repayment."

"You can meet Aleksandr," she offers carefully. "As long as we're not seen together in public. That's all I can allow."

"It's enough," I say, even though it isn't.

She exhales again, relief threaded with sorrow. "Thank you."

When the call ends, I don't move. Pushing her now would get me nowhere. I know her too well.

She needs to see it on her own.

That her life without me will be as empty as mine has been without her.

EIGHT

Anya

TWENTY YEARS *ago*

I LIVE out of suitcases now. Airports, hotel rooms, cold rinks that smell the same no matter what country I'm in. My name is printed on programs in languages I don't speak. I skate. I win. I bow. I fly again.

Somewhere between Helsinki and Toronto, I realize I've become successful.

Leo and I see less of each other because of it. Or maybe because of him. The business takes more of his time now. It always did, but it feels heavier lately, like it's pressing down on him from all sides. We're still together. We never say otherwise. We just... adjust.

He sends flowers to my hotel rooms, no matter where I am. Roses in Paris. Lilies in Tokyo. White tulips in Amsterdam.

There's always a note. Always my name in his sharp handwriting. He congratulates me on every win. He remembers dates better than I do.

Sometimes, when I skate in Moscow, I scan the audience out of habit, and there he is. Sitting still. Watching only me. I skate better when I know he's there.

We talk at least once a week. More when I'm injured or exhausted or emotional. I complain about my ankles, my knees, the bruises that never quite fade. He listens. He always listens.

He never talks about himself anymore.

I know why. After that night, when he showed me the gun and the truth, there were more wounds. More silences. Once, he was in the hospital for eight weeks. I flew back and sat by his bed, holding his hand while machines hummed softly around us. I never asked how it happened. He never offered.

I stopped asking questions that hurt us both. He worries I can't handle the truth, that it will affect my performance. Maybe he's right. Maybe I'm too fragile to be the girlfriend he needs, the comfortable place he requires. But he's still the most amazing boyfriend in the world. And I'm grateful every day. Even when I question myself, even when the lies and the quietness starts to make me wonder if I'm doing the right thing, I cling to him because I know that just me existing helps him. He has too many enemies. I'm his only friend, even though he prefers to call us lovers.

He's still tender with me. Still careful when it matters. The sex is the best of my life, fierce and grounding and intimate in a way that makes the world disappear. But he's quieter now. Rougher around the edges. Less boy, more man shaped by things I will never fully see.

This morning, I dress carefully.

Leo is picking me up. We're going on a real date for once. A nice restaurant. I asked for it because I miss him, because I miss us being normal for a few hours. He was wary, I could hear it in his voice, but he agreed. He always gives me what I ask for. Sometimes, I worry about that. I want to be there for him, too.

The doorbell rings.

When I open the door, my breath catches.

Leo stands in the hallway in a dark suit that fits him perfectly, tailored to his broad shoulders and narrow waist. His hair is neatly combed, a few brown threads catching the light. He looks older. His body is bigger, more muscled and broader. More handsome. He's powerful in a way that's quiet and dangerous.

"Hi," I say stupidly.

"Hi," he answers, and his eyes soften when he sees me.

He kisses my cheek, lingering just long enough to make my heart stumble. "You look beautiful. I missed you, malishka. You smell like sunshine."

"You look hot, too," I tease. "But who are you, and what have you done with your leather jackets?"

"They're still there," he says dryly. "I clean up occasionally."

He drives. One hand on the wheel, the other resting briefly on my knee at red lights. Small touches. Silent reassurances. We talk about nothing and everything. My last competition. His travel schedule. The weather. How we're both suddenly tired in ways we never used to be.

"We've changed," I say quietly, watching the city slide past the window.

"Yes," he agrees.

"But we're still us," I add.

His fingers tighten once on the steering wheel. "We are. We will always be."

The restaurant is opulent. Crystal chandeliers. Soft music. Linen tablecloths and low voices. The kind of place where people pretend not to stare at him and fail. Leo catches attention like he was born for it. I'm the world-famous figure skater, but nobody recognizes me when I'm beside him. He sucks up all the air in the room.

His aura of quiet danger and lethal sexuality has every woman casting him glances. I hold his arm possessively, staking my claim on him.

His mouth lifts in an amused smile. "Careful, malishka, or the lasers you're shooting from your eyes will kill them."

I kiss him on the cheek. "You're mine, Leo Antonov. And I am not hiding it."

He breathes deeply. "I love you when you're jealous."

"You love me even when I'm not jealous."

"Da." The single syllable is full of years' worth of feelings. It's all I need. Despite the challenges and us barely seeing each other, our bond is stronger than it used to be. Leo has been a stable rock, and his secrets make him more intriguing to me.

Even as the traces of the boy who dreamed with me vanish, I embrace and respect the man he has become.

I don't crave a past version of him. And he doesn't cling to the girl who ate too many piroshkies and dreamed of conquering the world. He loves the too-busy woman who sometimes falls asleep in the middle of a call, whose victories are followed by insecurities and brutal travel schedules.

We see each other's scars, and there seem to be more and more as time passes. Yet, it doesn't seem to matter.

He orders fast, and when our food arrives, I hurriedly try to grab a piece of fried potato and it spins as it lands on the table.

"I swear that spin was better than my triple axel," I remark. "Can't believe I lost to a piece of meat."

Leo grins; this time he shows teeth. For one second, it's like I'm back in the past, looking at the boy who used to laugh like it was the most natural thing in the world.

"When was the last time you smiled like that?" I ask gently.

"Too long," he says.

I study him across the table. The weight he carries is visible now, carved into his posture, his stillness. He's no longer wild. He's disciplined. Controlled. A man who commands rooms without raising his voice.

I like how the boy became this man.

"Do you hate me for changing?" he asks suddenly.

"No," I say without hesitation. "I love you more because you're complex. Because you're not always the same person. I like watching you transform." I smile softly. "I've changed, too."

"You haven't," he says. "You're still optimistic. Being with you still gives me hope."

The words warm me from the inside out.

When more food arrives, he lifts his fork and offers me a bite. I blush, aware of the glances around us, but I lean in anyway. I like that he isn't afraid to show affection. I like that he chooses me openly, even here.

We eat slowly. We're trying to prolong the time we have with each other. Once we leave, once we go back to our lives, I have to travel for a month. I don't know when I'll see him again, when we'll be able to spend hours leisurely soaking in each other's company.

After dinner, his hand settles on my back, steady and protective, as he leads me outside. The night air is cool. His car waits by the curb.

He walks toward it, but a sharp sound slices through the air.

I feel a sharp sting at the corner of my ear as something whizzes past. My heart jumps as Leo's eyes widen.

"Fuck. Someone shot you. Get down, Anya." He pushes me behind him, shielding me with his body, hugging me and pushing my back against the car. I hear another bullet.

A hard cry echoes through Leo's throat. Panic rises in my veins. Did he get shot?

There's pain in his eyes, sudden and fierce, and then his weight slams into me.

He collapses.

"Leo," I scream, catching him as he falls.

Blood spreads dark and fast across his shirt. Too much. Far too much.

I drop to my knees beside him, my hands shaking, my vision blurring as I press against the wound and beg him to stay with me.

"Leo, please," I sob. "Please don't leave me."

The world narrows to his face, pale under the streetlights, and the sound of my own heart breaking open.

NINE

Leo

ZORINA LOOKS resplendent up on the stage. It's her first concert after she gave birth to Mikhail's child, and now that she's back, Mikhail is swooning at her like a besotted husband.

"Isn't she beautiful?" he muses, holding their six-month-old baby in his arms. He's sitting beside me. He's the third-oldest and third-youngest Antonov, squarely in the middle. In his mid-thirties now, he looks like a polished Russian businessman as well as a doting husband and father. I'm glad he is happy now. He was always tormented before he married Zorina, refusing to believe in love and happiness. But she seems to have changed his outlook on life.

"Zorina was always beautiful," I reply. "That's why I arranged for you to marry her."

"It might be the best thing you've ever done for me," Mikhail admits.

A slight smile coaxes my lips upward. "Maybe I'll become a matchmaker after I retire."

Mikhail scoffs. "You? Retire? That's never going to happen."

I sigh. I've always lived for the family, for the organization. I had to let Anya go once, and since my parents died, I have done nothing but grow our empire. Throwing myself into work seemed to the be only way to forget about her and the fact that she was married to someone else. As news of her pregnancy spread in the media and she retired from figure skating, I became more closed-off and gave up hope on having anything more than money, titles, and authority.

But seeing Aleksandr and her again has me imagining a future I never thought I was worthy of. What if I could just be a man? A father, a husband?

I criticize myself mentally for being so idealistic. Even if I pass down the title of pakhan to one of my brothers, my old enemies will never forget about me.

"She's playing better than ever," Mikhail muses. He knows more about music than I do. Zorina always appreciates his input. I guess they're a good match.

The baby wriggles in his arms and he kisses the head, stroking its small back. "There, there. That's your mama. Isn't she fantastic?"

I look at his big hands engulfing his child and miss something I never had. Aleksandr would have been this small once, too. But it was Petrov's hands that held him, not mine. The same hands that now leave scars on the child's body.

"Take good care of him," I tell Mikhail. "Don't hurt him."

Mikhail frowns. "Of course I won't hurt him. He's my son."

"And the future heir of the Antonov empire," I say with authority. "He's the oldest son."

Lena is pregnant with a boy, but he hasn't been born yet.

Nikolai and Aleksei's firstborns are both girls. I know they'll have more children, so we'll have more options in the future. We have a lot of positions to fill, and while I'm not open-minded enough to letting the girls launder money like Dmitry, I don't want them involved in violence.

Technically, says an evil voice in my head, *Aleksandr is the oldest male child in the family.*

I push it away. I had no choice but to follow my father's footsteps and become a mobster. But I won't drag my son into the world of the Bratva. Anya won't let me. She's right. It's best if I stay away from him and let him lead a normal life. It's what I could never have. But I don't want to leave Anya again.

The dilemma has been weighing on me heavily: do I let her go so my son can live the quiet, normal life he deserves, or will I let my possessiveness and unquenchable desire ruin Aleksandr's life? Someday in the future, will I be teaching him how to hold a gun and kill people the way my father did to me? Is that the legacy I want to pass on?

A headache throbs behind my eyes. I rub my temples as the beautiful notes of Zorina's violin crescendo in the concert hall.

Mikhail's the only one of my brothers who got an arranged marriage. Zorina comes from a bratva family. Her parents were against her pursuing a career as a violinist. They wanted her to stay at home, have babies, and be a good Bratva wife. But Mikhail has been quietly supporting her dreams even before they got married.

After their engagement, he sent her to the best conservatory, and signed her to one of the record labels that he owns. He manages the 'legal' empire that the Antonovs own. Casinos, hotels, movie production, studios, music management, and similar businesses. Dmitry, my younger brother uses them to launder money sometimes,

I look around the hall, seeing as Anya quietly creeps in.

I came here to meet her. Her divorce is going to take a while to go through, but in the meantime, I need to check in on her, to make sure she's alright. I wonder if Petrov has been beating her more because she asked for a divorce. And if he did, it'd be my fault. I can't intervene without making it clear that I'm protecting her.

And if I do that, my enemies will know she matters to me. Here, in Moscow, I have more eyes on me than in Las Vegas. I have to make every move strategically, or the people closest to me will get hurt.

I lean closer to Mikhail and lower my voice. "I'm going to the bathroom."

He nods absently, eyes locked on the stage, his attention wholly consumed by his wife and the music pouring from her violin. I doubt he even registers that I stand.

I move quickly through the aisle, head down, phone already in my hand. One message to Anya, brief and coded. *Women's restroom. Five minutes. I've handled it.*

The cleaner waits outside the restroom exactly where I told her she would. I press folded bills into her palm as I slip past. "No one comes in," I say quietly. "Including you."

She already has a 'cleaning in progress' sign outside the restroom, but I ask anyway. "Is anyone inside?"

"Nyet," she replies. "Gospodin Antonov. I know who you are. I wouldn't dare."

The door closes behind me. The lock clicks. Silence settles, thick and private. It's a luxurious bathroom, at least by public restroom standards.

The space smells faintly of lavender. The cleaner must have wanted to impress me. Her son owes Aleksei a debt, and he seems to have fallen behind on some payments. I know she wants me to go easy on the boy. She seems to have freshened up the place nicely, scrubbing every tile clean. I doubt she works this hard every day.

I wait, checking for messages from Igor, answering the ones I can. The drug trade never stops, not even for a second.

Then I hear it. The soft, precise sound of heels on tile. I turn as the door opens again.

Anya steps inside. She's wearing white. A wool coat, pristine and elegant, and beneath it a satin dress that clings to her like it remembers every curve. She looks unreal. Fragile and luminous, like something carved from light.

And then I see the cut.

It runs along her cheekbone, angry and red, too visible even under careful makeup. Rage detonates in my chest. I feel the heat spreading through every cell of my body, making me burn with something I haven't felt in ages.

"Who did that?" My voice is low and dangerous as I cup her face. "Was it him?"

She gives a humorless smile. "No. Men from the Bratva, obviously. Who did you think?"

My hands curl into fists. She sways slightly, just enough for me to notice. She's not even walking straight. Did he hit her leg, too? My anger sharpens into something colder.

"Take off your coat," I order. "I need to see what that bastard did to you."

"Leo—"

"Now."

She exhales and shrugs out of the coat. She folds it over her arm with careful movements. When she steps closer, she surprises me by wrapping her arms around my waist.

She's trembling.

"Hold me," she whispers, voice cracking. She looks up at me, showing me her deepest vulnerability. Her eyes are filled with tears. I can tell that she's on the edge of despair, and all I can do right now is to steady her, to embrace her and reassure her that I'm there for her. "Please."

I guide her down, lowering the toilet seat before I sit and pull her onto my lap. Her weight settles against my chest. I stroke her hair, slow and steady, grounding us both.

"I expected him to react badly," she murmurs into my collar. "But at least he didn't refuse the divorce. Your lawyer must have scared him. He was irritated. He called me ungrateful. Took it out on me."

I swallow, jaw tight. "Show me where else you're hurt."

She shakes her head. "No. I look ugly. I don't want you to see me like this."

"I will never think you're ugly," I say immediately. "You're always gorgeous to me."

Her fingers tighten in my jacket. "Just like you never told me what you were doing when you joined the Bratva to protect me, I want to protect you. Seeing it would hurt you."

"I have seen dead bodies, bleeding men, and ugly corpses" I say. "I have a strong stomach."

"No." She shakes her head. She lifts her head and looks at me. "Don't be. Today made me realize how bad it's gotten. I should have left years ago." Her voice steadies. "Thank you. I couldn't have done this without you."

"Thank Aleksandr," I tell her. "He asked for help first."

She leans in and whispers against my ear, "Your son takes after you. He's fearless and reckless. Like you used to be."

I huff a dry breath. "You must hate that."

"I love it," she says simply. "It feels like I have a part of you with me all the time. That's what gives me strength."

My chest tightens. "Where is he?"

"With the maid," she answers. "He's watching the show."

She hugs me harder, then kisses me. It's desperate. Needy. I know she's hurting more than she's letting on.

My hand skims her waist. She winces.

"What's wrong?" I ask sharply.

"I think he broke a rib," she admits. "Or cracked it."

"Did you go to the hospital?"

She shakes her head. "He never allows it. He doesn't want proof."

The fury comes back, blazing and uncontrollable. "I'm taking you now. We'll collect evidence. We'll make sure this ends cleanly."

"Don't bother. He agreed to the divorce anyway. And I'm sure it'll heal. It always does." The resignation in her tone stings. I can't believe she thinks this is normal. I'm a mobster, and a lot of men in crime beat up their wives like it's nothing, but I don't condone the misuse of violence. The golden rule in the Bratva, or the yakuza, or any other organized crime outfit is that we can never touch a civilian. Only debtors and rival gangsters. Normal people like her are not part of our world and must never become the target of our violence.

"I want you to get the best care. Get checked out by proper doctors. It might be more serious than you think." I settle my hand on the small of her back. "Don't argue with me, malishka. Come."

She looks up at me, eyes shining. "You care too much. I'm deadweight to you. I can't return your kindness, but I'm clinging to you because you're the only man who makes me feel safe. You're this huge, tattooed gangster. Your name terrifies people. But you're the only person I feel comfortable sharing horrible truths with."

She locks her arms around my neck, pressing her breasts against my chest.

"You're not a deadweight," I say firmly, stroking her back. Having her breasts smooshed against me, her weight leaning against mine, is its own kind of pleasure. I have longed for this simple joy for a decade. It's not that she needs me. But she trusts me, enough to bare her darkest secrets, enough to let herself depend on me. "I want you to share everything that's happening with me. That's exactly why we're meeting like this."

She swallows. I hear her throat move. Her breathing frays as she suppresses a sob. "You know; I've been thinking about about what I could give you in return for your generosity."

"I want nothing—"

She silences me by placing a finger on my lips. Her pupils are blown wide, intent and unmistakable. "You do want something. And until the divorce is final, I'm ready to give it."

Understanding hits me like a blow, especially when she shifts on my lap, running her fingers along my jaw sensually.

"Do you mean—"

She nods. "My body is yours for these few months. You can do whatever you want with it, however many times you want. I can't stay after. But while we keep it secret, I want you. I'm tired of being faithful to a man who thinks I'm his punching bag."

"Are you sure, malishka? You don't have to feel obligated."

"More sure than I have ever been," she replies, resting her forehead against mine. "I love you, Leo, even after all these years. When you fucked me that day, I realized how much I craved you. My dreams of you at night...those were pale imitations of the way you made me feel when you came inside me. So don't you think I'm sacrificing myself. I'm not a saint. I desire you. I know we're star-crossed lovers, that we won't end up together. We never do. It's always something or the other—my career, your father, my safety, our son. So I want to treasure the time that I can have with you."

I kiss her, slow and restrained, pulling back before I lose control. "We're going to the hospital first."

She nods again. "Okay."

I stand and lift her into my arms. She curls into me without protest as I carry her out, the weight of her words settling heavy and electric in my chest.

Her offer will haunt me.

I already know I'm not strong enough to refuse it. Aleksandr's safety rests on me staying away from her. But I can't leave unless I've had my fill of her, unless I've had her in all the ways I've desired.

All I hope is that a few months will be enough to make me forget about her forever so I can do the right thing for my son.

TEN

Anya

TWENTY YEARS AGO...

THE HOSPITAL SMELLS like antiseptic and fear.

I've been sitting in the same chair for hours, my hands clasped so tightly my fingers ache. The ICU doors are closed, unforgiving, their narrow glass window the only mercy. Through it, I can see Leo lying still, tubes and wires threading into him like something mechanical has taken over where his body failed.

They took the bullet out. The doctor said he was lucky. I don't believe in luck. I believe in prayer.

I prayed while he was in surgery. I prayed when the blood soaked through my hands as I pressed on his wound in the street. I prayed when the ambulance doors slammed shut and I couldn't climb inside fast enough.

I really thought he was dead.

But he's breathing now. His chest rises and falls. God must have been listening.

My phone vibrates in my palm. I don't want to answer it. I already know who it is.

"Anya," my agent snaps the moment I pick up. "Why aren't you at the airport?"

"I can't come," I say. My voice breaks. "My boyfriend was shot. I'm at the hospital."

Silence, then a sharp exhale. "You're joking."

"I'm not." Tears spill down my face. "He almost died."

"This is exactly what I warned you about," he says coldly. "That man is trouble. You have Hungary tomorrow. You need to qualify if you want Worlds this season."

"I don't care about medals right now," I shout, startling a nurse down the hall. "He got shot saving me. I'm not leaving him."

"You're being emotional," he says. "Careers don't survive emotions."

"He's the love of my life."

"That gangster?" he scoffs. "He's not worth sacrificing everything you've worked for."

"You don't know anything about him," I snap. "You don't know what he's done for me."

"If you don't get on a plane in two days," he says, voice turning hard, "you forfeit this season. And a comeback next year might be impossible."

I press my forehead to the glass, watching Leo sleep. "Then I forfeit."

The line goes dead.

I slide down in the chair and cry silently, my shoulders shaking. *I'm so sorry, Leo. I never should have asked for that date. You kept me away from public places for a reason, and I was too selfish to see it.*

"I'm sorry," I whisper through the glass. "Please wake up."

I don't know how long I stand there, crying and pressing my fingers against the cold glass, hoping for a miracle.

Heavy footsteps echo down the corridor disrupts my concentration. This area of the hospital isn't busy, so the sound startles me.

I look up.

The man walking toward me looks like violence given a body. Black coat. Heavy boots. His face is a map of old scars. I recognize him vaguely from photographs Leo never explained.

"Who are you?" he asks.

"Who are you?" I shoot back, standing.

His mouth curls. "Are you the ice ballerina my son has been seeing?"

"I'm a figure skater," I correct sharply. "And you haven't answered my question."

"I'm his father." His eyes flick to the ICU doors. "And you're an idiot for bringing him here."

My stomach drops. "I was trying to save his life."

"You brought him to a civilian hospital," he says, contempt dripping from every word. "Now the police will ask how a bullet got into him. Because of you, he's going to be questioned. And I'll have to clean up this mess."

"I didn't know," I whisper.

"Of course you didn't." He steps closer. "Leave. I'll have him moved to our doctor."

"He's in intensive care," I protest. "That's dangerous. You should wait until he wakes up."

I glance backward at Leo sleeping peacefully, unaware that his brutal father is trying to drag him away. I feel anger and powerlessness rise inside me as his dad ignores me, instructing his men who barge into the room.

When I try to block his way, he shoves me aside.

"Stay out of my family's business," he says roughly. "Or I'll make sure my son wakes up to your corpse. He doesn't need you, and I don't like the sight of you."

My blood runs cold.

"You're a nuisance," he continues. "An ordinary girl has no place with him. I'll make sure he breaks up with you."

"He loves me," I say, shaking. "We love each other."

He laughs. "Then marry him."

My heart stutters. Marriage? We have never discussed that, but right now, I'm too young. I have more seasons left in me.

"If you marry him," he continues, enunciating every word slowly, "you will have to give up your public career. You'll have to devote your life to him. There's no divorce in the Bratva. You belong to him until death."

"I'm young," I say weakly. "We haven't talked about marriage. I mean, in the future, when I retire…I might marry him."

I see his expression transform then. He was irritated but now he looks disappointed. He tips his chin up, looking down on me like he was right about me all along.

"Those are just excuses. The truth is that you never will be ready," he says flatly. "You're a coward. You're scared because you saw what life with him will be like. When the excitement of having a boyfriend wears off, you'll break his heart. You can't walk in the darkness beside him. You're too weak."

"I'm not weak. I'm giving up World Championships for him," I cry. "I'm staying here until he opens his eyes."

"That hesitation," he says, eyes hard, "tells me everything. Go skate. You'll never be what he needs. He will never be what you need, either. So cut your losses while you're ahead. Think of this as a learning experience."

"I'm not leaving him!" I get in front of the door. "And I'm not letting you take him. He should get treated here."

This time, he isn't patient. His hand flashes out. He slaps me. Pain explodes across my cheek. The shock of the impact makes my knees buckle. My butt hits the ground. My body burns with the aftershocks of that slap.

"Learn when to quit," he snarls.

His men grab me. I scream Leo's name, fight them with everything I have, but they drag me away from the ICU, my cries swallowed by the walls.

TWO DAYS LATER, I'm in Hungary. I couldn't stay with my uncle and aunt. I didn't even know where Leo was, and being in Moscow made me feel unsafe. Especially after his father threatened me. So I took a flight to Budapest, because it was the only escape.

The hotel room is silent. My phone rings. It's the lady at the reception, telling me she's connecting a caller to me.

"Anya." Leo's voice is hoarse but alive. Just hearing him makes my body sag with relief. He's alive. He's okay. He's talking to me. His voice sounds weak and raspy, but at least he survived.

Tears rush to my eyes pouring down my cheeks in hot, shameless streams.

I sob. "I'm so sorry. I put you in danger. Thank goodness you're alive."

"It's my fault," he says. "I should've let you go sooner."

"No," I beg. "Please. I know what your father said, but I love you."

"We're done," he says gently. "I want you safe. I wish you the best with skating."

My chest caves in. "Promise me something," I whisper. "If I make the final at Worlds, come watch me skate."

A pause. "I promise."

"Promise me I won't see you again," he adds. "I don't want to hurt you."

I swallow. "I promise."

The line goes dead.

I sit on the edge of the bed and cry, knowing we still love each other.

And knowing that sometimes, love is not enough.

ELEVEN

Leo

ANYA CALLED me because she had no other option.

She had a meeting with the lawyer. Her nanny was unavailable. Aleksandr was home from school. She hesitated before asking, and I heard it in her voice. She didn't want to impose. She never does.

"I thought," she said carefully, "that he might like spending some time with you."

I said yes before thinking it through. Mostly because I wanted to erase her troubles.

Now I'm standing in her apartment, hands in my pockets, wondering what one does with a ten-year-old boy when one has spent most of one's life avoiding softness.

Aleksandr looks up at me like I'm Christmas morning.

"You came," he says, wide-eyed.

"So it seems," I reply.

He grins and bounces on his heels. "Mama said you might be too busy to babysit me."

"Life is full of surprises." I can't believe it myself. I know I should approach Aleksandr carefully. I'm still just a stranger to him. And I'm not sure what to talk about with a kid. I should have turned down Anya's offer. But I couldn't help wanting to find out what my son was like. Not that knowing will make it any easier to let him go when the time comes.

"I'm glad you're here," he agrees solemnly, like an old man trapped in a child's body. "You're better than Svetlana. She's always angry."

Anya leaves after kissing his hair and giving me a look that is equal parts gratitude and warning. When the door closes, silence drops.

Aleksandr studies me. I study him. He's dressed in a plain blue T-shirt and pajamas. He has a curious look in his eyes, and I haven't even finished that thought before he starts grilling me like I'm being interrogated by the police.

"So," he says. "Are you really a gangster?"

"No," I answer flatly.

He squints. "You look like one."

"Unfortunate genetics."

He laughs, then sobers. "Thank you for making my mama leave my papa."

I stiffen. "That wasn't my doing."

"Yes, it was," he insists. "After you came, she cried and then she packed things. Papa yelled, but she didn't listen anymore."

I say nothing. There are truths I do not correct.

"Do you miss him?" I ask instead.

He shakes his head without hesitation. "There's nothing to miss. He never spent any time with me. Only when he hit me for getting bad grades or talking at the dinner table."

That lands heavier than it should. I put my hand on his

head, ruffling his hair. It's soft, and this small touch feels like something more than I deserve.

"My mama says we'll move to my grandparents' house when the divorce is done," he continues. "I don't know them very well."

"They're good people," I say.

He considers that, then asks, "Why can't we move in with you?"

My heart kicks hard enough to hurt.

"Why me?" I manage. "You don't know me well. We just met twice."

"You're strong," he says simply. "I'd feel safe. And you talk nicely to my mama. She smiles when you're around."

"She doesn't smile around me," I say before thinking.

"Yes, she does," he replies. "She smiled before she left today."

He's right. She did. She also kissed my cheek when he wasn't looking.

I don't argue.

He wanders the apartment while talking, asking questions like they're items on a checklist.

"Do you really have a house in America? Uncle Anatoly told me you're rich."

Anatoly, that bastard. Is he the one who told Aleksandr that I was rich and powerful? He has been shooting off his mouth too much.

"Da," I reply, drily. I want this questioning to end, but I can't tell Aleksandr to shut up, and I don't know how to distract a boy his age. I don't have any cool stories or gadgets—none that are appropriate for children.

"How big?"

"Too big."

"Is America cool?"

"It's loud. People smile too much."

"That sounds fake."

"You have no idea."

He nods, satisfied, then asks about my family. I answer what I can. I avoid what I cannot. He's innocent, and I'm awkward around innocence because I'm used to the dark, cold hearts of men who have been trained for violence.

Finally, I turn the tables. "What are you interested in?"

His eyes light up. "Guns."

I can't help scoffing. Of course he's interested in guns. He's my son.

"When I grow up," he says, "I want to do something where I can shoot them."

"That is a terrible idea," I tell him.

"Unless I'm a police officer?" he offers, knowing how adults think. He's already so clever. He knows what people around him want to hear and tells them exactly that.

The idea of my son being in the police is laughable, though. Someday, will he catch me?

I snort before I can stop myself. "The police aren't that great. They don't pay much. You'll be poor all your life."

He beams. "Yeah. The bad guys are more fun. They're stronger. And richer. Like you."

"Is that what you think I am?" I ask quietly. "A bad guy?"

He shrugs. "I heard at the party that you're Bratva. That's why I asked you for help."

I crouch and put my hands on his shoulders. "That word is not a good word. You should never approach anyone from the Bratva. They can hurt you."

He nods, serious now.

Then his gaze drops to my jacket.

"What's that?"

I follow his eyes. Damn it. He just noticed the gun I'm

carrying. Of course I carry one everywhere. I'm a walking target.

He gets closer, touching it before I give him permission to. "Is that a real gun?" His eyes twinkle with glee. "Can I touch it? Please? I'll be careful."

I should probably refuse. But Anya isn't here to scold me.

"Don't pull the trigger. And listen to me." I unload the gun carefully, checking twice, then hand it to him grip-first.

His awe is immediate. Reverent.

Fear curls in my chest. He's too familiar with it. Too interested. I'm already feeling like I failed a parent. I should have kept him away from guns, not given him a real one to check out. I grab the gun from his grip hurriedly and shove it back into my coat.

"That's enough. You shouldn't like guns."

"But I do."

"Don't you want to be a figure skater like your mama?" I ask.

He scrunches his nose. "You think I can? I can't even balance when I'm standing on flat ground. Mama took me to an ice rink when I was younger, but I kept falling."

"Nothing is easy at first," I tell him. "But figure skating is a respectable profession."

"Is that what you want to do?" he asks, as if challenging me.

"I did want to be a skater when I was young," I confess. "For a brief moment. When I first met your mama. But I wasn't good at it, either."

He nods like he understands. He watches me too attentively, like he's expecting me to spill the secrets of the universe. I try to get him to watch TV to end the barrage of questions, but he says he's more interested in talking to me. He's definitely not a normal kid. What normal kid picks their parent over screen time?

After I switch off the television, I try to lure him with the promise of hot chocolate, but he doesn't want it.

"What do you want, then?" I ask, exasperated.

He looks up at me and asks the question that splits the room in half. "Are you my real father?"

The air leaves my lungs. For a moment, my mind goes blank. I wasn't prepared for this.

"Why would you think that?" I ask, clearing my throat awkwardly.

"Because you said it to my mama that night," he says. "You were angry. I heard you."

"That isn't true," I say quickly. "I'm not your father."

"You look like me," he argues. "You protect us. You like guns, too."

"Coincidence," I say, forcing steadiness. "Your father is Petrov."

He studies me for a long moment, then his shoulders sag.

"If you were my dad," he says softly, "I think I'd be happier."

My heart races. I just don't know what to do in a situation like this. I can't get my emotions under control, but my poker face has been perfected over decades, so it doesn't give anything away.

"You wouldn't. I'm not a good father. I get bored of kids. I am very strict." I clap my hands. "I sent my brother to a boarding school in England because he got in trouble at school. I'm coldhearted."

"You're better than my papa who hits me and mama." He sighs, a sigh that is too mature for a ten-year-old. "With you, we could live in a big house in America and I could learn to shoot guns. My life would be more fun if you were my papa."

Something breaks.

I pull him into my arms before I can stop myself. He

freezes, then relaxes against me, small and warm and impossibly mine.

For one stolen moment, I let myself pretend. "Aleksandr," I tell him softly. "I'm not your father. Don't ever tell anyone that I am, okay? You will be in danger."

"Because you're a gangster?" he asks, still not giving up on that line of inquiry.

"Because I have enemies," I reply. "And they're very bad people. Even worse than Petrov. They would shoot a real gun at you if you told them you knew me. So never tell anyone you talk to me. Understand?"

For the first time, fear flickers in his eyes. They're blue like Anya's, and I hate to see them tremble with terror. But this is another way I protect him.

He finally nods, "Okay," and I hug him tighter.

TWELVE

Anya

SIXTEEN YEARS AGO...

I DIDN'T PLAN to meet him again. I mean, what are the chances of running into a mobster at a luxury hotel in Las Vegas?

Leo Antonov sits at the bar, the sharp angles of his handsome face illuminated by the mood lighting, looking like a Hollywood movie star. The kind of guy who picks up women with nothing more than a look.

When he glances at me, my lungs stutter. His gaze slams into me like an ice storm, freezing my limbs, making sure I can't run from the intensity of his gray eyes. He looks so cold, so...broken. Even more than I remember. He's the same age as me, but the lines on his face are deeper, like he has lived more than me in the same span of time.

I walk up to him, rubbing my eyes, trying to convince myself that I'm not dreaming. I never saw him again after we broke up. I threw myself into figure skating. I had a slump after an injury last year. I thought my career was over. But I made a brilliant comeback this year, sweeping the Worlds. And now I'm spending a well-deserved vacation in America, a place I've always wanted to visit.

I was planning to gamble at the casinos after grabbing an expensive cocktail in the hotel's bar. I was steeling myself with liquid courage because I'm not the risk-taking type.

"Leo? What are you doing here?" I ask. "I thought you were still in Moscow."

"I own this place," he replies, dropping that bomb casually. He looks older than before, but it's not just the age. It's the way he carries himself. Like a powerful, important man. Not a restless gangster obeying the commands of his father. "Well, technically, Mikhal owns this place. But it's the same thing."

"Your brother Mikhail?" I ask in disbelief.

"Yes, Malishka." There's a note of impatience. "We bought it with money from our illegal activities. Are you satisfied now?"

There's animosity in his voice. It rings out clearly, making me feel unwanted and unwelcome. I know he's just trying to push me away. He got shot because of me and I never got a chance to make that right with him.

"I thought your papa would never let you leave Moscow," I murmur.

"He's dead," Leo answers flatly. "My parents died in a car crash last month."

Last month. I inhale as pieces click together.

"Is that why you didn't come to see me at the World Championships?" I know everything isn't about me. He probably forgot the promise he made me. It has been four years, after all.

But I looked for him in the audience that day, my heart racing, hoping against hope that he'd be there. That I could ask him to be my boyfriend again, tell him I was ready to marry him, settle down, and retire because I had already achieved everything I set out to do.

It would have been the perfect romantic reunion—jumping into his arms, gold medal hanging around my neck, kissing passionately, lovers reunited. But I wore the medal to my hotel room, where I cried alone. Victory felt hollow without him, without someone to celebrate it with.

"I'm sorry," he says, and the heaviness in his tone suggests that he means it. "I broke my promise."

"Then I should break mine, too," I say, putting my hand on his. I brush my thumb over his, feeling the broken nail and the rough texture of his skin. A shiver crawls up my spine. I like that he's still untamed, that touching him still makes my spine tingle the way it always did. "Leo, if your father is dead, we have no reason to not be together anymore."

Leo laughs. "You want to be with me? After you got shot? After you're successful? Didn't you learn your lesson last time?"

I drag my fingers up his jaw. "I was scared before, Leo, but I've missed you too much to be scared again." I swallow as his pupils dilate. His jaw tightens a friction as I feather my finger over it. "Can I show you something? You'll have to come up to my room to see it."

His eyes narrow in suspicion. "You have a funny way of seducing a man, Malishka."

"I'm not seducing you." Heat bursts into my cheeks. "I mean...if you want...we can...do that...but I wanted to show you something else."

He doesn't budge. How silly of me. I assumed he might still

love me, still want me like I want him. But what if the years have changed him? They certainly seem to have hardened him into a man whom I barely recognize.

"Do you have a new girlfriend? Is that it?" I ask.

"That's none of your business," he replies gruffly. "I can do whatever I want. We're not together anymore."

The bar is dimly lit, the air thick with the scent of expensive liquor and quiet conversations. Leo's presence fills the space, commanding and imposing. I push myself closer to him, squeezing into the space between his bar stool and the counter. His eyes are stormy, conflicted, but I see the spark of desire in them, the same one that's always been there when he looks at me.

"You're avoiding the question," I say, leaning in so close that my breath mingles with his. "Is there someone else? Someone who makes you feel the way I did?"

He leans back slightly, his gaze drifting over my face, lingering on my lips. "Why does it matter to you?"

"Because," I say, my voice barely above a whisper, "I want to know if I have a chance. If there's a place for me in your life again."

He takes a sip of his drink, his Adam's apple bobbing as he swallows. "I don't have a girl. I'm too busy looking after my younger siblings," he admits, his voice rough. "I was just trying to blow off some steam at the bar before you interrupted me."

I take that as my cue. I slide onto his lap, feeling the hard muscles of his thighs beneath me. He chokes on his drink, coughing slightly, but he doesn't push me off. I take that as a sign that he needs me, that he wants me as much as I want him.

"You need more than alcohol to blow off steam," I murmur, cupping his face in my hands. His stubble grazes my palms, sending a thrill down my spine. "Let me help you."

His hands find my hips, squeezing firmly, possessively. My pussy clenches in response, a rush of heat and desire pooling between my legs. I can feel him getting hard beneath me, his cock pressing against my ass. I grind against him, eliciting a low growl from his throat.

"What are you doing, Anya?" he asks, his voice a mix of warning and longing.

"Making you feel good," I whisper, my lips brushing against his ear. "There's been no one else for me, Leo. No one but you. I've never stopped loving you."

His grip on my hips tightens, and I can feel his cock swelling beneath me. I reach down, stroking him through his pants, feeling the hard length of him throb under my touch.

"You don't have to torture yourself," I say softly. "If we're both single, we can do whatever we want."

He frowns, his eyes darkening. "You've become too forward, Malishka."

"I don't care what people think anymore," I confess, my voice thick with emotion. "I cared too much before, and I lost you. I won't make that mistake again. I can make you feel good. Come with me."

I brush my lips against his, feeling the electric spark between us. He grits his teeth, murmuring my name like a curse and a prayer. "You'll regret this."

"Make me regret it," I challenge, my heart pounding in my chest.

My challenge ignites his competitiveness.

He grabs my wrist and stands up, dragging me to the elevator. Once inside, he asks, "Which floor?"

I press the button, my heart racing. The doors close, and he pushes me against the wall, his body pressing into mine. I can feel his hard cock against my stomach, and it makes me wet, my pussy throbbing with need.

When we reach my floor, he throws me over his shoulder. I hand him the key card, and he carries me into the room, tossing me onto the bed. I crawl onto all fours, grabbing his shirt as he tries to leave.

"I'll suck you off," I say, my voice breathless with desire. I barely got him here. I can't let him leave.

His eyes widen, a mix of shock and hunger in his gaze. "Anya…"

"Please," I beg. That softens him. He hesitates, pausing for a moment. That is enough time for me.

I slide off the bed and onto my knees, looking up at him with a hunger I've never felt before. His eyes are dark, filled with a primal need that sends a shiver down my spine. I reach for his belt, my fingers trembling slightly as I unbuckle it. He watches me, his breath hitching as I slide his pants down, followed by his boxers.

His cock springs free, thick and hard, the tip already glistening with precum. I've never done this before, but the sight of him, the scent of his arousal, makes my mouth water. I reach out tentatively, my fingers wrapping around his shaft. He's so thick that my fingers barely touch, and a thrill of excitement and nervousness shoots through me.

I lean in, my tongue flicking out to lick the tip. He groans, a deep, guttural sound that sends a wave of heat straight to my core. The taste of him is salty and masculine, and I find myself craving more. I lick him again, this time letting my tongue explore the length of his shaft.

"Fuck, Anya," he growls, his fingers tangling in my hair. "You look so fucking good on your knees."

His words send a jolt of pleasure through me. I open my mouth, taking the head of his cock between my lips. He's big, and it takes a moment to adjust to the feel of him in my mouth.

I swirl my tongue around the tip, listening to his groans of pleasure.

"That's it, malishka," he murmurs, his voice rough with desire. "Take me deeper."

I do, inch by inch, feeling him fill my mouth completely. His fingers tighten in my hair, guiding me, setting the pace. I relax my jaw, letting him slide deeper, gagging slightly but pushing through it. The sound of his groans, the way his hips buck slightly, drives me wild.

"You're such a good little cum slut," he praises, his voice a mix of tenderness and filth. "You take my cock so well."

His words should shock me, but they only serve to heighten my arousal. I moan around his cock, the vibrations making him grunt in pleasure. I bob my head, sucking him harder, faster, my hand working the base of his shaft in tandem with my mouth.

I hollow my cheeks, sucking harder. He groans, his fingers digging into my scalp, gripping tightly as he controls the pace.

"That's it, Malishka," he growls, his voice rough with desire. "Suck me hard. Be my dirty cum slut."

I take him deeper, feeling him hit the back of my throat again. His grunts and moans fill the room, and I feel a rush of pleasure knowing I can make him feel this good. He moves my head up and down, fucking my mouth with deep, powerful thrusts. The friction from his cock bumping against the back of my throat makes my brain go numb every time. It's a powerful sensation that stops my breath and stills my body for the brief instance while it lasts.

"You want my cum, don't you?" he rasps. "Suck harder. Show me how much you want it."

I do, taking him as deep as I can, feeling my throat constrict around him. His grip on my hair tightens, and he begins to move my head, shoving his cock inside me faster, his hips moving at a quicker pace.

I can feel him getting closer, his cock swelling in my mouth, his breath coming in short, sharp pants. Tears are leaking from my eyes, trailing down my cheeks. My vision is blurry from the sting at the back of my throat. But I want to give Leo everything I have. Including my pain.

"I'm going to come down your pretty little throat," he growls. "And you're going to swallow every last drop like the good girl you are."

The first spurt of his release hits the back of my throat, and I swallow reflexively. He groans, his hips jerking as he comes hard, filling my mouth with his salty essence. I swallow it all, the taste of him overwhelming but intoxicating.

When he finally pulls out, I look up at him, my lips swollen and wet. His eyes are filled with a mixture of satisfaction and disbelief. We stay like that for a moment, our breaths mingling, the intensity of what just happened hanging heavy in the air.

His thumb presses against my cheek, wiping away my tears. "You don't look pretty when you cry. I'm sorry."

He dabs the cuff of his shirt against my other cheek, soaking away the moisture spilling down my eyes. My pussy is way wetter, though. My thighs feel uncomfortably sticky, coated in my own arousal. But I don't care about my own pleasure today.

Then I ask him, my voice soft and vulnerable, "Were there any other women? In the years since we broke up?"

He looks at me, his eyes filled with a mix of desire and regret. "Not one."

"And you?" he asks, his voice husky. "Were you with anyone else?"

"No one," I admit. "I couldn't stand the thought of another man touching me."

And in that moment, it's clear. We've never gotten over each other. The years, the distance, the pain—none of it matters. We're still here, still drawn to each other like magnets, still incapable of letting go.

The room is silent, the weight of our confessions hanging in the air. But in that silence, there's a spark of hope, a promise of something more. We still love each other, and maybe, just maybe, that means we have a chance to start again.

THIRTEEN

Leo

"WHY DID you want me at the airport?" Anya asks, breathless, as if she rushed here on instinct alone.

"Why did you want me at the airport?" Anya asks, breathless, as if she rushed here on instinct alone.

The private terminal is quiet in a way public airports never are. No lines. No crowds. Just polished stone floors that reflect soft ceiling lights, glass walls looking out onto the tarmac, and the low, constant hum of machinery somewhere beyond sight. The air smells faintly of coffee and jet fuel. A place built for people who do not wait.

She stands a little too close to me, coat still on, hair slightly undone from hurrying. Her cheeks are flushed from the cold. From nerves. From me.

"I'm taking you on a date," I say.

Her brows knit together. "A date?"

"Yes."

She lets out a soft, incredulous laugh. "Where, on the tarmac?"

I straighten my spine. That's usually a good way to let people know I'm serious. "America."

That makes her laugh properly. The sound hits me low in the chest. "You're insane. I didn't even pack a bag."

"You don't need one," I reply. "I'll buy you clothes and whatever else you need."

She stares at me, searching my face. "That's generous," she says slowly. "And completely reckless."

"Both can be true. Besides, I wanted our date to be special. I don't have much time with you, Malishka. I'm not going to play it small."

I take her hand. Not possessively. Just enough to feel her there. Her fingers are cool, but they curl into mine without hesitation. For a second, we simply stand like that, neither of us speaking, the world moving quietly around us. I feel the weight of what I am doing settle into my bones. This is not impulse. This is intention.

I want to give her the kind of extravagant luxuries I couldn't give her before. We always dated in secret, hiding like we were committing a crime. Technically, while she's separated, she's still married to Petrov, so I thought it'd be better to go somewhere nobody would follow us to. I doubt Petrov's private investigators—if he has hired any—would follow us to another continent.

"You could have taken me somewhere nice here," Anya says. "Moscow has plenty of places."

My mouth tightens. "Don't you remember what happened the last time I did?"

She exhales, the humor draining from her expression. "We both got shot."

Memory flickers in her eyes. The day I took her out years

ago. The gunshot. The blood. The lesson that carved itself into both of us.

"Yes," I say. "And Moscow hasn't become any safer since."

She nods, because she knows this already. "So that's why," she murmurs. "Why you never take me anywhere public. Why it's always apartments, empty buildings, closed spaces."

"It's the only way I can keep you safe here."

Her thumb brushes over my knuckle, absent, thoughtful. "You shouldn't have to live like this."

"I do," I say simply. "Being a pakhan means making sacrifices. But I get to live in luxury, so I can't complain too much."

We move quickly through a private corridor. The airport hums beyond glass and steel, distant and irrelevant. Security nods. Doors open. The jet waits.

Inside, everything is quiet wealth. Cream leather. Polished wood. Soft light. I shrug out of my coat and help her with hers, fingers lingering at her wrist longer than necessary. She wears a pale blouse and dark trousers, simple and elegant, her hair pinned back. I am in black, tailored and severe, the uniform that keeps me alive.

A flight attendant offers a warm towel and asks for her drink preference.

"Water," Anya says automatically, then turns to me. "Leo, where in America are we going?"

"To a place that means something to us," I say. "Las Vegas."

Her breath catches. Her eyes close for an instant, like she's recollecting the past. We have memories in that place. In so many places. We've had a long association. "That's hours away."

I brush my hand against the headrest of the seat. "It's the weekend. I have business there."

She swallows. "And what about Aleksandr? I thought this

was going to be a quiet date, so I told the nanny I'll be back in a couple of hours."

"He's coming with us."

Before she can respond, footsteps approach. Small, quick steps. Sneakers slapping softly against stone. A familiar rhythm that sends something sharp and unguarded through me.

The attendant returns, guiding a small figure down the aisle.

"Mama!" Aleksandr's voice rings out, bright with wonder. Anya turns just as Aleksandr appears from the corridor, jacket half-zipped, eyes already drifting past us toward the windows. His excitement hits the room before he does.

Anya gasps. "Sasha."

"Is that a plane?" he asks, pointing. "Is that ours?"

She laughs despite herself. "Aleksandr."

I watch him take it all in. The space. The height. The quiet authority of the place. He looks at me, curiosity sparking instantly.

"Did you bring me here?" he asks, skipping toward me. His eyes are shining as they meet mine. "I knew you were cool."

Having my soon call me cool is a different kind of experience. Nobody thinks I'm cool. Dangerous, lethal, rich…sure. But none of those are what people aspire to be.

I ground myself as it feels like he ground is tilting slightly beneath me. Aleksandr looks around, tapping his leg restlessly.

"I take it that you've never been on a private jet before," I say.

"It's so cool," he replies. "Do you own it?"

"Yes."

"Do you own more planes?"

"Da."

"How many?"

"Enough."

"Can it fly really fast?"

"You'll find out when we take off."

Anya presses a hand to her forehead. "You cannot interrogate him like this. Sit down, Sasha."

He grins, unrepentant. "I like asking questions."

"I've noticed," I remark drily.

He resembles Dmitry in that way. My younger brother, who is in college and launders money for the organization, used to be a curious kid like Aleksandr. He was always asking questions. It irritated me back then, because I had no interest in being a patriarch or father-figure. I was focused on surviving, on making enough money so we could afford a good life in America. But after raising Nikolai and Dmitry for nearly two decades, I have become more patient.

"It's time to put on your seatbelt." The flight attendant walks over, giving me a nod, implying that the pilot is ready for takeoff.

Aleksandr listens to her as she lets him have the biggest seat beside the window. Anya and I take the one opposite him, separated by a wide, carpeted expanse.

I watch Aleksandr's nose pressing against the glass, awe stealing his voice into silence.

Other jets wait outside, sleek and white, engines still. Power held in check.

I look at Anya, who is smiling at her son. To know that I gave her this small moment of happiness sends a wave of joy through me.

"Thank you for thinking of Aleksandr," she says. "I didn't think you'd bring him."

Anya rests her fingers over my palm. The touch, so warm and freely given, makes heat curl under my fingers.

"Why wouldn't I?" I keep Anya's hand in mine as long as I can, closing mine over it so she can't remove it from my grasp.

This is dangerous. Stupid. Reckless.

And I have never been more certain of anything in my life. I have only a few months to make memories to last a lifetime, so I can't cut corners.

Anya looks at me again, softer now. "You surprise me every time."

"In a good way or a bad way?"

Her lips curve. "In a good way."

FOURTEEN

Anya

SIXTEEN YEARS *ago*

AFTER LEO FUCKS ME AGAIN, we lie tangled together in the hotel sheets, our bodies slick with sweat, our breathing slowly returning to normal. The room smells like sex and us, a heady combination that makes my head spin. I trace patterns on his chest, feeling the steady thump of his heart beneath my fingertips.

"Leo," I whisper into the darkness. "Can I be your girlfriend again?"

He stiffens beside me, and I feel his hand still where it's been stroking my hair. "Anya..."

"Please," I interrupt, my voice cracking. "You don't know how miserable I've been without you. Every night, I'd lie in bed and wish I could call you, just to hear your voice. After I got injured last year, I had constant breakdowns, performance anxiety that nearly destroyed me. If you had been there, I would have had someone to talk to. Someone who understood."

His arm tightens around me. "But you got through it on your own. You're strong, Anya. You don't need me."

I push myself up on one elbow, looking down at his face in the dim light filtering through the curtains. "But I want you. I don't want to live a life where I can't be with the man I love. Your father was against our relationship, but he's gone now. We can be together."

His jaw clenches. "Are you ready to be shot at again? Because that's what being with me means. It's more dangerous now than it was before."

"I'd do anything to be with you," I say fiercely. "A bullet is nothing compared to the emptiness I've felt without you."

He shakes his head. "You say that now, but you'll change your mind. Things are more dangerous now that I'm pakhan. I have more enemies, more responsibilities."

"I won't change my mind," I insist. "I've been miserable without you. I regret breaking up with you every single day. I want to be yours, Leo. I know you're a gangster, and I don't care."

His eyes search mine in the darkness. "I won't get hurt again, Anya. I can't. So don't start something unless you're sure you can marry me and be a bratva wife. Can you handle that? Can you handle living in the darkness beside me for the rest of your life?"

I'm riding high on my victory, on the recklessness that comes from finally getting what I want. I've fulfilled my dream of winning the championships. "I'll probably skate another year or two. Then I'll quit and be with you forever. I don't need the fame or the money. All I want is a quiet life with you, building a family, waking up in your arms every day. You're in America now—there isn't the same level of danger anymore. We can be together and live a life of freedom."

He sighs, gazing at the ceiling. His eyes look dead and hopeless. "A lot of the work I handle is still in Russia. I'll be going back and forth between the two countries. I might eventually settle down in Russia permanently, leaving my brothers to look after our business in America."

"Then I'll follow you anywhere you go," I say, hugging him tightly. I kiss his collarbone, then trail kisses down to his chest, my lips moving through the dark hair there. "I think a love like this only comes once in a lifetime, and I want to take a chance on it."

He cups my face in his hands and pulls me up for a kiss. His lips are soft at first, tender, before the kiss deepens. His tongue slides against mine, claiming, possessing. I moan into his mouth, my body already responding to his touch.

When he pulls back, his eyes are intense. "You better keep this promise, because my heart isn't strong enough to endure another breakup with you."

His hands move to my breasts, drawing circles over my areolae before pinching my hard nipples. Pleasure knifes through my core, igniting a flame in my belly. I shudder as his rough skin slides over my sensitive peaks, stimulating me with slow, teasing brushes. My pussy clenches at the tender yet abrasive touch. Moisture leaks out of my channel. The heat in my stomach grows and expands like a monster growing heads.

I've just had sex, but Leo can turn me into a needy, horny woman with no real effort.

"One day," he murmurs, cupping my breast. "these will be filled with milk to feed our baby. Your tits will be huge, and swollen. Because I'll put a baby inside you, Anya. I'll make you a mother."

I shiver under him, a rush of arousal flooding through me at his words.

His eyebrow raises. "Did that turn you on, malishka?"

I blush, nodding. "Oh my God. Yes."

A predatory smile crosses his face. "Then maybe I should fuck you while you're wet. Get started on making those babies."

He runs his hand between my legs, his fingers coming away glistening with my arousal. I can't pretend his words didn't have an effect on me. I have loved Leo for years. The idea of growing his child in my stomach fills me with a surge of warmth. I want to create a family with him, make sure we're bound to each other for life.

Leo strokes my slick pussy lips. His calloused fingers are like a match striking against my throbbing pussy. He sets me on fire with every contact. I drop arousal onto his hand, consumed by the poisonous heat swirling inside me, begging to be put out.

"You're such an eager breeding slut, getting this wet for me." The words are dirty and brutal whispered against my ear. Just what I'd expect from a gangster. But the mere idea of fucking a man as dangerous and powerful as Leo Antonov is a turn on. He'll fill my channel with cum just like he filled my mouth. And I'll take every drop because all I've ever wanted was to be his.

"I'm on birth control pills," I admit breathlessly. "I can't afford to get my period during competitions, so nothing will happen even if you fuck me raw."

His eyes darken. "You shouldn't have said that. Now I'm going to pump you full of cum, since there won't be any consequences."

He grabs my legs, pulling them apart and tossing them over his shoulders. The position opens me completely to him, making me feel vulnerable and exposed. His cock, already hard again, presses against my entrance.

"Leo," I gasp as he pushes inside in one smooth thrust.

He groans, his hands gripping my thighs. "Fuck, you're still so tight. Your body is perfect, Anya."

He starts moving, his thrusts deep and deliberate. Each stroke sends waves of pleasure through me, making my toes curl. The angle with my legs over his shoulders lets him go so deep, I can feel him everywhere.

"You take my cock so well," he growls, his fingers digging into my thighs. "Like you were made for me."

I moan in response, unable to form words. The pleasure is overwhelming, building with each thrust. He leans forward, folding me nearly in half, and the new angle makes me cry out.

"That's it, malishka," he encourages. "Let me hear you."

He pulls out suddenly, flipping me onto my hands and knees. Before I can catch my breath, he's pushing back inside, the position allowing him to go even deeper. I feel the thick head of his cock stretching me, filling me completely.

His hands grip my hips, holding me steady as he pounds into me. The sound of skin slapping against skin fills the room, mixed with our heavy breathing and my moans.

"Your pussy grips me so well," he says, his voice rough with arousal. "It's begging for my dick."

His words send a shiver through me. One of his hands slides around to my front, finding my clit. He rubs it in tight circles, the dual sensations of his cock and his fingers pushing me closer to the edge.

HE DOESN'T GIVE me time to adjust, setting a brutal pace that has me crying out with each thrust. The angle is deep, hitting spots inside me that make stars burst behind my eyelids. His fingers dig into my thighs hard enough to leave bruises, and I love it.

"That's it," he growls. "Take my cock like a good girl."

The bed creaks beneath us, the headboard slamming against the wall with the force of his thrusts. The sounds of our bodies coming together—wet, obscene—fill the room along with our moans and gasps.

"Harder," I beg, my hands fisting in the sheets.

He complies, his hips snapping against mine with bruising force. The pleasure builds inside me, a tight coil in my belly that winds tighter and tighter until I'm trembling on the edge.

"Leo," I gasp. "I'm going to—"

"Not yet," he commands, slowing his thrusts. "I want to feel you come around my cock when I fill you up."

He pulls out again, and I whimper at the loss. He lies back on the bed, pulling me on top of him. I straddle his hips, sinking down onto his cock with a moan. This position lets me control the pace, and I start riding him, my breasts bouncing with each movement.

His hands come up to cup them, squeezing and kneading. "These are going to get even bigger when I knock you up," he says, his eyes dark with lust. "They'll be so pretty."

The image sends another wave of arousal through me. I ride him harder, chasing my pleasure. His hands move to my hips, helping me move, guiding me up and down on his thick shaft.

"That's it," he groans. "Ride my cock. Take what you need."

I lean forward, changing the angle, and suddenly he's hitting that spot deep inside that makes me see stars. I cry out, my movements becoming erratic as pleasure builds.

"Close?" he asks, his thumb finding my clit again.

I nod frantically, unable to speak. He rubs my clit in firm circles, his other hand gripping my hip to help me maintain the rhythm.

"Show me how much you need me," he commands. "Show me who owns your pussy, who makes you come like a slut."

His thumb finds my clit, rubbing tight circles, and I shatter. My orgasm crashes over me in waves, my pussy clenching around him rhythmically as I scream his name. Again and again, until my throat is hoarse and the pleasure he filled me with starts to evaporate.

Before I can come down from my high, he flips us again. I'm on my back, my legs spread wide as he kneels between them. He drives back into me, his thrusts becoming harder, more desperate.

"Fuck, I can feel how deep I am," he groans, pressing a hand to my lower stomach. "My cock is touching your womb. Right here, where our baby will grow."

His words make my still-sensitive pussy clench around him. The pressure of his hand on my stomach combined with the feeling of his cock so deep inside me is overwhelming. I can feel every inch of him, stretching me, filling me completely.

He angles his hips, hitting my cervix with each thrust. The sensation is intense, bordering on painful but somehow pleasurable at the same time. His free hand finds my clit again, rubbing it with practiced precision.

"You're going to take all my cum," he says, his voice strained. "I'm going to stuff you until you're full. It'll be leaking out of you for days."

The dirty talk combined with the physical sensations pushes me toward another orgasm. I can feel it building, coiling tighter and tighter in my core.

"Leo," I gasp. "I'm going to come again."

"Then come," he commands, his thrusts becoming even more forceful. "Milk my cock with that tight pussy while I breed you."

The pressure on my stomach increases as he leans forward,

changing the angle again. His cock seems to swell even larger inside me, stretching me impossibly wider. The slight pain mixed with pleasure sends me over the edge.

My second orgasm hits even harder than the first. My pussy clenches rhythmically around his cock, trying to pull him deeper. I feel myself gushing, my arousal coating both of us.

"Fuck, yes," he groans. "That's my good girl. Take my cum. Take all of it."

His thrusts become erratic, losing their rhythm as he chases his own release. I can feel his cock pulsing inside me, can feel the warmth as he fills me with his seed. He buries himself as deep as possible, his body shuddering as he empties himself inside me.

He doesn't stop. His hands grip my hips, pulling me back onto his cock with each thrust as he empties his balls inside my pussy. He shoots load after load of cum into my unprotected cunt, filling me with his seed.

"Look at you," he says roughly. "Taking my cock so well. You were made for this, weren't you? Made to be bred by me."

"Yes," I moan, pushing back against him. "Breed me, Leo."

He reaches around, his fingers finding my clit again, and delight thrums through my veins. My arms are giving out so my face presses into the mattress. The angle shifts, and he groans, his thrusts becoming erratic. But he continues to give me every inch of his hard dick, continues to shove his cum deeper into my pussy until sticky fluid clings to my inner walls, coating them in his potent release.

He stays buried inside, grinding against me as he empties himself completely.

When he finally pulls out, I can feel his cum starting to leak down my thighs. He flips me onto my back, spreading my legs to watch it drip out of me.

"Even if you change your mind and betray me," he whispers

in my ear, his voice dark and possessive, "I'll put a baby inside you. No matter where you are, your body is mine. You're the only woman I can imagine having children with."

The words should scare me, but instead they send another wave of heat through my exhausted body. I pull him down for a kiss, tasting the promise and the threat in his words.

"I won't change my mind," I whisper against his lips. "And it's not just my body you own. My heart is yours, too."

I see his eyes grow misty. It has been ages since I saw him so emotional. I guess envisioning having a family with me is making him sentimental, even if it won't happen for a while. After all, he still has his brothers to consider.

"I love you, Anya." He squeezes my ass. "And I'm afraid you're right—you might be the only woman I'll love in this lifetime. But I'm glad it was you."

He holds me close, and in the quiet aftermath, I know I've made the right choice.

FIFTEEN

Leo

THE BAR LOOKS SMALLER than it did in my memory, but everything does once time has had its way with you.

The lighting is warmer now, amber instead of blue. The mirrors behind the shelves have been replaced with smoked glass. The place used to lean into excess, velvet and neon, the kind of luxury that wanted to be seen. Now it feels controlled. Expensive without trying. Mikhail's hand is all over it.

"It doesn't look the same," Anya remarks, with a wistful note in her voice.

"Mikhail still owns it," I tell her. "He renovated a few years ago. Said the old place looked like something that belonged in the previous century."

She takes it in slowly, eyes moving over the polished wood, the marble counter, the low murmur of voices. "I can't believe it's been sixteen years," she says. "It feels...impossible."

"It felt like fate back then," I admit. "I was trying to forget you. And then you walked in. I thought I'd seen a ghost."

She smiles at that, soft and sad at once. "I thought it was destiny, too. I'd just won. I was finally ready for a relationship. And there you were."

We take seats at the counter. Leather stools, worn smooth by years of elbows and secrets. I nod at the bartender, who recognizes me without surprise. Old habits linger.

I help Anya out of her coat, sliding it off her shoulders and draping it over the back of her chair. Her skin is warm beneath my fingers. Bare. Familiar in a way that never faded.

"You're more beautiful now than you were then," I say quietly.

She blushes, looking down as the drinks arrive. "You always say dangerous things like that."

"They're only dangerous because they're true."

She takes a sip, then looks at me over the rim of her glass. "You never told me anything back then," she says. "Not really. When you got shot, I realized I didn't know what your life actually looked like."

I watch the ice melt in my drink. "Most of it would have turned your stomach."

"That's not why you didn't tell me," she says. "You were afraid I wouldn't love you anymore."

I meet her gaze. There is no point lying now. "Yes."

She exhales. "I would have loved you anyway."

"Knowing I killed people brutally?" I ask.

"Yes."

The word lands clean. No hesitation. She looks at me, not blinking. I can sense her resolve. I guess being with Petrov has changed her view of things. In the past, I don't think she'd have said the same thing.

I change the subject before I lose my grip. "Your parents. How are they?"

"They're old," she says with a small smile. "But they're well. Still in the same town. Still arguing about the weather."

"Have you told them about the divorce?"

"No. I won't until it's final."

I huff a quiet laugh. "That means I'm the only one who knows."

She lifts her glass. "Congratulations. You're trusted."

It warms me more than the alcohol.

She tilts her head. "You barely existed when we got back together," she says gently. "I felt like I saw you less then than when we were teenagers."

"I was holding everything together with my teeth," I say. "After my parents died, the organization nearly collapsed. I had four brothers to protect and enemies who smelled blood."

She listens. Always did. But in the past, I never gave her the chance to be the listener. Never shared my troubles with her. Maybe I ought to change that, too.

"Dmitry was almost kidnapped once," I continue. "The Sokolov Syndicate had our shipments seized at the St. Petersburg port. I slept in my office for weeks. Every decision felt like it could get someone killed."

"And I was asking you to come to dinner," she says softly.

"Yes."

She hesitates, then asks the question that has waited years between us. "Is that why you let me go? When I broke up with you?"

The memory hits like cold rain.

My office back then had been all steel and glass. Gray sky pressing against the windows. Phones ringing nonstop. Reports spread across my desk. Dmitry missing for six hours. Men calling from the port. Money bleeding out of every corner.

She had stood there, hands clenched, eyes bright with unshed tears.

"I can't do this anymore," she had said.

And I had answered, without looking up, "Da."

I swallow and take a drink. "I was drowning," I say now. "And I didn't have the strength to fight for you that day. All I could think about was survival."

Her fingers brush my wrist. "You asked me to marry you later."

"Yes."

"And I said no."

"You'd already chosen Petrov."

The rejection had been quiet. Polite. Final. It had hollowed me out more than any bullet ever did.

"I was lonely," she says. "You were always working. He was charming. Present. And when I left you, you didn't even argue."

"I would change that," I say. My hand tightens on her shoulder. "If I could do it again, I would fight."

She leans into the touch, just slightly. Enough.

We sit there, the bar humming around us, time folding in on itself. Past and present pressed close.

"You're still here," she says.

"So are you."

And for the first time in years, it feels like we might finally be standing in the same moment.

"Do you want to..." Leo hesitates. He points upstairs. "Get a room?"

I laugh. "I never thought I'd see the day when Leo Antonov is shy about asking to fuck me." I press my hand against his shirt, feeling the thumping of his heart. He must be anxious because it's beating fast. "Yes, I want to get a room. That's why I volunteered to pay you with my body for all your troubles."

Her hand stays on my chest, and I feel the heat of it through the fabric. My heartbeat kicks harder, and I know she feels it.

"You're not paying me with anything," I say, voice low. "I don't want your body as payment."

Her eyes flash. "Then what do you want?"

"You," I answer simply. "All of you. Your heart, soul, body. Not a transaction. Not because you feel guilty or because you feel grateful. But because you want me."

The words hang between us, raw and exposed. She searches my face, looking for the lie, the angle. She won't find one.

Her expression softens. "Okay," she whispers. "I'm sorry. I didn't mean it like that. I desire you, Leo. I want to be intimate with you again. How could I not? When you took me in my apartment that day…I felt you between my legs for days afterward. Every time I was with Petrov, I felt my pussy sore and throbbing from stretching around your fat cock. God, it was so good. Satisfying."

I grip her face. "I love when you talk dirty. Especially when it's about my cock."

Her lips tick up in a smile. She scoffs. Is she surprised at how much I love making her admit that she needs me, even if it's just my cock? I need all of her, though. Her mind, body, soul, heart, and her willing submission.

"I didn't realize how much I missed good sex," Anya admits, licking her plump lips. Just the sight of them, wet and juicy, makes my cock jerk in anticipation. I end up remembering how she made me lose control when she sucked my cock years ago, in this exact hotel. She leans against me, placing her hands on my shoulders for support. Her eyes are clear. No doubt. No hesitation. Just lust and need. Just the way I like it. "My marriage with Petrov was lonely. I know you must have thought a lot of things when we were apart, but let me assure you: we never had sex except in the first few months. He never wanted to touch me. Once I gave birth to a son, and he had the heir he wanted, he didn't need my body. After that, he completely lost interest in me. He had younger, beautiful women to satisfy him. I was only his wife in name."

"I'm so sorry." I press a soft kiss to her chin. "But at the same time, I'm not sorry at all."

She coughs out a laugh. "You're so possessive."

"Not just possessive," I reply. "I'm glad he didn't touch you. Because he didn't deserve to. Given the way he hit you, he had no right to be near you at all."

"No, he didn't." Anya cups my face. Her touch sends a wave of electricity through my system, making me feel alive for the first time in years. "But you do."

I can't help myself, even if we're in a public place. There's nobody except the bartender. I angle my face downward, capturing her lips in a slow, reverent kiss. Her lips, full and wet, are pliant. I suck on them, drinking in her moans.

I muffle her cries with my mouth, plunging my tongue into her depths. Heat scorches the side of my tongue where it brushes hers. I bracket her face with my hands, rubbing my fingers over her soft skin, making her moan and cry until she's breathless and has to pull away.

"Leo, we shouldn't be doing this here," she says.

"You're right." I hold her hand. The sense of deja vu is instant. I took her hand and dragged her to her hotel room in the same way sixteen years ago.

At least the electric chemistry and passion between us hasn't changed.

I stand straighter, pulling her against my body. The bartender doesn't look up as I leave cash on the counter—too much, but I don't care. My hand finds the small of her back as we move toward the elevators. The lobby is quiet, tasteful. Mikhail's renovations made everything feel like controlled luxury. The scent of clean, expensive perfume fills my nostrils.

The elevator doors close, sealing us in. I hit the button for the top floor. Penthouse suite. Always kept available for family. Back then, it was a luxury we didn't have. Now we do.

Anya turns to me, her back against the mirrored wall. "Are you nervous?"

"Yes."

She blinks, surprised by my honesty. "Why?"

"Because it's been sixteen years," I say. "Because last time I had you, I thought it would be forever. I'm terrified because this is temporary again. And when you leave me, I'll never be able to come back to this place again."

Her hand cups my face. He eyes narrow in sadness. I think she understands how much she affects me. "Leo..."

I catch her wrist, pressing a kiss to her palm. "It's okay, malishka. I'm a grown man. I know what you offered, and I'm ready to face the future, even though I know you won't be in it."

"I wish I could be." For the first time, she looks up at me with tears in her eyes. It catches me off guard, igniting my buried protective instincts.

"Why are you crying, Anya? You changed you mind?"

She shakes her head, wiping the trail of tears trickling down her cheeks. "You think this is easy for me, Leo? You think I want to keep leaving you? When we met again at Anatoly's daughter's engagement, all I wished was to be with you forever. I wished I could choose you. Leaving you hurts me more than you imagine. I know that I will be alone for the rest of my life, because I cannot love another man breaks my heart. But if I'm selfish, if I choose to marry you, and something happens to Aleksandr, how would I forgive myself? I would live with self-hate forever."

I understand it is a difficult decision. That's why I accepted her decision to be with me until her divorce comes through.

"I will protect you both," I murmur. "I cannot guarantee that he will never be harmed, because death and injury are realities everyone accepts in my line of work."

"I know," she says. "And you know, I never told you this, but these last few years, I was always so scared that something would happen to you. That one day, I'd receive news from someone that you were gone. It kept me awake at night."

"Yet, here I am, completely fine." I spread my hands, turning around to show her how fine I am.

She punches my chest playfully. "You're just lucky."

"No, I have a lot of good people around me. Not that long ago, someone tried to kill me during a meeting. Do you know who stepped in and saved me?" I pause. "Aleksei's wife."

Anya inhales sharply. "But she's a woman. And wasn't she pregnant?"

"She's a brave one," I say. "I was suspicious of her at that time. She was an American and Aleksei was too smitten with her. But she proved how much she cared about Aleksei and me. She threw herself in front of him like a shield to save him—and me, by extension."

"Like you did for me once?" Anya's eyebrow twists upward.

"We all make sacrifices for the ones we love." I rub my jaw. "So the reason I've survived all these years is not because of luck. It's because I'm surrounded by people who love me, and who love each other."

Anya's shoulders relax an inch. "I'm glad you have so many people who love you."

"And if you marry me, they'll love you, too." I inhale, breathing in the perfume clinging to the air. "I see the way you are right now. You have nobody who loves you. Your husband abuses you. Your son depends on you. You need good people around you."

She doesn't say anything, and she doesn't have to.

The elevator dings. Doors slide open.

I lead her down the hall, keycard already in hand. The suite opens to floor-to-ceiling windows overlooking Moscow, the city sprawling in lights below us. But I don't look at the view. I only see her.

She steps inside, turning slowly, taking in the space. Modern. Clean lines. A massive bed dominating the room.

"It's beautiful," she murmurs.

I close the door, lock it. The sound echoes.

She faces me, and I see it—the uncertainty mixed with want, the way her breath comes faster, the slight tremble in her hands.

"Come here," I say.

She crosses to me, and I pull her close, my hands sliding up her back. I bury my face in her hair, breathing her in. She still smells the same—something floral mixed with cold air and skin.

"I missed you," I admit against her temple. "Every fucking day."

Her arms wrap around me, tight. "I missed you too."

I pull back just enough to look at her. Then I kiss her.

It starts soft, testing, like we're learning each other again. But that lasts maybe three seconds before hunger takes over. My tongue slides against hers, and she moans into my mouth. The sound goes straight to my cock.

I walk her backward toward the bed, my hands already working the buttons of her blouse. She's fumbling with my shirt, pulling it free from my pants. When her fingers touch bare skin, I groan.

"Off," I growl, tugging at her clothes.

She helps, shrugging out of her blouse, reaching behind to unhook her bra. It falls away, and I stop breathing.

"Fucking beautiful," I mutter, my hands coming up to cup her breasts. They're fuller than I remember, heavier. Perfect. I thumb her nipples, watching them harden into tight peaks. She gasps, arching into my touch.

"Leo, please..."

"Please what?" I ask, lowering my head to take one nipple into my mouth. "What exactly are you begging for?"

She cries out, her fingers threading through my hair. "Please shove your big dick into me and stretch my pussy so I can feel you for days."

I bite down gently, then soothe with my tongue. "Godness, you have a filthy mouth, malishka."

But I'm not patient either. Not when she looks ravishing and ready to be devoured. Her nipples are ripe and firm. I lick them slowly, sealing my mouth around her areolae one by one, making her moan. Then I strip her quickly, efficiently, until she's bare before me. Then I step back to look. "Turn around."

She does, slowly. I can see the faint scars Petrov left on her skin, and rage flares hot in my chest. I push it down. Tonight isn't about him. Tonight is about us.

"On the bed," I command. "Hands and knees."

She climbs onto the mattress, positioning herself. The sight of her like that—ass in the air, pussy already glistening—makes my cock throb painfully. Her cunt is slick with arousal, pretty like a rose.

I strip off my own clothes, watching her watch me in the reflection of the windows. Her eyes go wide when she sees my cock, hard and ready.

"You remember how big I am?" I ask, stepping closer.

She nods, biting her lip.

"Every inch of my big dick is going to be inside your pussy

in a few seconds. You'll be stretching so much for me. Enough for me to fill you with cum." I kneel behind her, running my hands up her thighs.

She shivers. I spread her legs wider, exposing her completely.

"So wet already," I murmur, running a finger through her folds. "Did you miss my cock, Anya?"

"Yes," she breathes.

I push one finger inside her, then two, feeling her clench around me. She's tight. So fucking tight.

"You haven't been fucked properly in years, have you?"

"No," she admits. "I miss it so much."

The words snap something inside me. I pull my fingers out and line up my cock with her entrance.

"Then let me remind you how it feels to be properly fucked by a gangster."

I forcefully shove my cock inside in one hard thrust. She cries out, her back arching, her pussy gripping me like a vice. Her velvet walls are like a prison, so soft, massaging my cock.

"Fuck," I groan, holding still to let her adjust. "You're squeezing me hard. I can feel how desperate your cunt is for me."

She's panting, her fingers clutching the sheets. "Move. Please, Leo, move."

I do. I set a brutal pace, my hips slamming against her ass with each thrust. The sound of skin on skin fills the room, mixed with her moans and my grunts.

"That's it," I growl. "Take my cock. Show me how much you missed it."

She pushes back against me, meeting each thrust. Her pussy is so wet I can hear it, can feel her arousal coating my cock.

I reach around, finding her clit. I rub it in tight circles, feeling her tense.

"Your pussy was made for my cock. I fit so perfectly." And her womb was made to take my seed, too. I knocked her up even though we had sex unprotected once on her wedding night.

And I'll probably knock her up again this time, even though she's much older.

My mind goes blank as she moans. Her pussy convulses hard around my shaft, squeezing me so hard, I have to fight for self-control. She is orgasming, and I have barely even started.

I grip her hips hard, my nails biting into her flesh. "Are you coming so fast? Fuck, your pussy must be horny for me."

I'm not done with her yet.

I pull out, ignoring her whimper of protest. I flip her onto her back, spreading her legs wide.

"I want to see your face when you come again," I say, pushing back inside.

This angle is deeper, and I can see every expression that crosses her face—the pleasure, the overwhelm, the love.

I fuck her hard, my hands gripping her hips to hold her in place. Her breasts bounce with each thrust, and I lean down to suck one nipple into my mouth.

"Leo," she gasps. "I'm going to—"

"Not yet," I command. "Hold it."

She whimpers, her pussy fluttering around me. I can feel my own orgasm building, my balls drawing up tight.

I reach between us, rubbing her clit again. "Now," I growl. "Come now."

She screams, her second orgasm even stronger than the first. The feeling of her pussy clenching rhythmically around my cock sends me over the edge.

I bury myself as deep as I can go and come hard, filling her with pulse after pulse of my release. It seems to go on forever, my cock jerking inside her as I empty myself completely.

When it finally stops, I collapse on top of her, both of us breathing hard. I roll to the side, pulling her with me so we're facing each other.

"Stay," I say, brushing hair back from her face. "Stay with me tonight."

She smiles, tired and satisfied. "I'll stay as long as you want me."

"Forever, then," I murmur, pulling her closer.

She doesn't argue. She just curls into me, her head on my chest, her hand over my heart.

And for the first time in sixteen years, I let myself believe that maybe, just maybe, we'll make it this time.

SIXTEEN

Anya

SIXTEEN YEARS *ago*

THE BATHWATER IS hot enough to fog the mirrors, steam curling lazily toward the ceiling. Leo sits behind me, long legs bracketing mine, his chest a solid wall at my back. His arm is draped around my waist, heavy and possessive without trying to be. The rhythm of his breathing matches mine after a while, like we've always known how to do this part.

I trail my fingers through the water, watching the ripples lap against the porcelain. "I want to date you again," I say, because if I don't say it now, I might talk myself out of it.

He doesn't tense. He doesn't laugh. He tightens his arm slightly, like he's anchoring us both.

"You can't change your mind after I say yes," he says.

"I won't." I turn my head enough to see his profile. The

lines around his mouth soften when he looks at me like this. "I know you're busy. We're both adults now. I won't ask for dinner dates or public things. I learned my lesson last time."

His brow furrows. "You shouldn't have had to learn that lesson."

"Maybe," I say. "But I did. And I still want you."

He exhales, a sound that feels like relief. "I need an escape sometimes," he admits. "From everything. And you make me forget about all the sordid things I do."

"I wish I could do more for you," I say, smoothing the crease between his brows. "You look like you've aged ten years in five. But be honest with me. Don't shut me out this time. If work is bad, tell me. If you're tired, tell me. I don't want us to be one-sided."

He nods slowly. "I'll try."

We sit with that promise between us, fragile and precious.

"I'm going back to Moscow tomorrow," he says after a moment. "When will you be back in Russia?"

"Two weeks," I answer. "Then I start preparing for the next season."

He smiles, small and proud. "You did it. You became a champion."

Warmth spreads through me that has nothing to do with the water. "I used to dream about this when I was a girl in a sleepy town. I can't believe I actually got here."

"I knew you would," he says.

I laugh softly. "You always had more faith in me than I had in myself."

"And you had too much faith in me," he replies, amused. "You really thought I could be a figure skating champion."

I twist slightly, splashing him. "You could still be."

He snorts. "After a year at the rink, I was still falling on my ass. Some people aren't meant for some things."

I turn in his arms and kiss him, slow and sure. "But we're both meant for this."

The intimacy of it settles deep in my chest. I haven't let myself be this open in a long time. Not with anyone.

"Oh," I say suddenly, remembering. "I need to show you my gold medal. That's why I invited you up in the first place."

His arm tightens around my waist, pulling me closer. "You can show me later," he murmurs. "Right now, I just want to hold my girlfriend."

My cheeks heat, and I duck my head, smiling into his shoulder.

Girlfriend.

For now, for this moment, that feels like everything.

SEVENTEEN

Leo

MIKHAIL'S HOUSE glows like a small palace at night.

Lights glow low behind tall windows. The gates open without pause, recognizing my car, and we drive up a curved stone path that could belong to a museum rather than a home. The mansion sprawls across the hill, all clean lines and quiet wealth, with enough rooms that even secrets can have their own space.

Anya's thighs tremble as she walks beside me through the entry hall.

I notice. Of course I do.

A slow, satisfied smile tugs at my mouth. I did that. I fucked her hard and made her come multiple times. Now she can't even walk straight. I leave my hand at the small of her back, not steadying her, just reminding her that she's not alone.

"I don't have any clothes to change into," she murmurs. "And Aleksandr doesn't either."

"We'll manage," I say calmly. "Besides, I'm sure my clever sister-in-law already has done something about it. Never underestimate Zorina."

Mikhail and Zorina come out of the living room to meet us. They're barefoot, dressed for the night. Mikhail wears loose dark pants and a thin T-shirt that does nothing to hide the fact that he's built like an armored door. Zorina is wrapped in silk, pale and soft, her hair loose down her back. Even half-asleep, they fit together effortlessly. She leans into him without thinking. He presses a kiss into her hair as naturally as breathing.

Their baby must be asleep upstairs or one of them would be holding. him. The house feels different because of it. Quieter. Anchored.

Aleksandr comes running and hugs Anya. She holds him close, kissing him on the head. "You're back," he says to her.

Then he tilts his head toward me. "And you, too."

There's something slightly accusing in his eyes, and I'm not sure whether he thinks I fucked his mother or thinks I let her play with guns and left him out of it.

He peels himself away as Anya yawns. "So, what did you do? I hope you didn't make trouble for Ms. Zorina and Mr. Mikhail."

Zorina's eyes flick to Anya, then to Aleksandr, and she smiles. "Not at all. He was so well-behaved. We went shopping together."

Anya arches her eyebrow at Aleksandr. "Shopping?"

"She bought me clothes, mama," Aleksandr replies.

"I figured that since you arrived with no bags, and Leo said you'd stay for a few days, I should make sure he had enough to wear," Zorina says lightly.

Anya blinks. "You did?"

"I hope you don't mind," Zorina says.

"Not at all. I'm so grateful. That was incredibly kind of you. I thought we'd use any old clothes you have."

Zorina laughs. "I mean, you can wear my clothes because we're around the same size. But I don't think any of them would fit Aleksandr. Besides, he was very serious about choosing things himself."

Aleksandr puffs up at that. "I picked the blue ones."

"They're very good choices," Zorina says solemnly.

Anya's voice softens. "Thank you. I will pay you back."

"You're Leo's guest, which means you don't owe is a thing. Also, I enjoyed it," Zorina replies honestly. "My son will be Aleksandr's age soon enough. I'm just practicing." She turns to Anya again.

Anya exhales, relief written all over her face. "I appreciate it so much. I was worried he'd start to grumble if he stayed inside all day."

Zorina gestures toward the stairs. "Come on. You must be exhausted. I'll show you to your bedroom. You guys can change into pajamas."

She takes Aleksandr's hand, already chatting with Anya as they head up together. Something about bedtime routines. About what Aleksandr liked when he was younger. Two mothers discussing about their trials. I can see a bond forming already, and I'm proud of the way Zorina manages to integrate everyone into the family. Their voices fade as they climb, weaving easily, like this arrangement makes sense to them.

I stand there longer than I mean to, watching their backs retreat.

Mikhail notices.

"That," he says dryly, "is not something I see every day."

I glance at him. "What?"

"You," he replies. "Smiling like that."

I scoff, but he's not wrong.

He folds his arms, studying me. "I must say; everything about this is unusual. You bringing a woman I've never met. Asking Zorina and me to take her and her son in. What exactly is going on? Do I need to expect danger? She was wearing a wedding ring. She must be married. But from the way you both looked at each other, she's clearly fucking with you. What have you gotten yourself into, Leo?"

I sigh, the weight settling back onto my shoulders where it belongs.

"We need to talk." I stiffen my shoulders, trying to look authoritative. I know Mikhail is not questioning my decisions, simply asking me for more information so he can decide what to do about security, but the need to be obeyed without questions is too deeply entrenched in me.

His expression sharpens, business snapping into place beneath the domestic calm. "Not here. The study?"

"Yes."

I straighten, walking with the posture that comes with the title I still carry. Whatever is happening with Anya, whatever this means for me, for the future, I am still the pakhan.

And Mikhail deserves the truth.

I turn toward the study, already bracing for the conversation that's been waiting years to happen.

"SHE'S PETROV'S WIFE." My voice rings in the huge, empty study. I drew the curtains already, and they keep out both light and sound. I don't want our conversation to be overheard.

Mikhail freezes mid-step. The decanter pauses above the glasses, amber liquid catching the light. "Petrov?" He frowns. "The name sounds familiar."

"He's a politician in Russia," I say. "They're in the middle of a divorce. Separated already."

Mikhail sets the decanter down carefully, like he's buying himself time. "Do you want a drink?"

"Yes." I could use some alcohol. Fucking Anya has me feeling both soaked in pleasure and exhausted.

He pours two fingers of whiskey into a glass and slides it across the table to me, then fills his own. He doesn't drink yet. He studies me instead.

"So," he says slowly, "are you having an affair with her?"

"My personal life isn't part of this discussion."

His jaw tightens. "Is the boy part of the discussion, then? Because I'd say it becomes relevant when a child is involved. What does he think of his mother being with a man who isn't his father?"

"I am his father."

The words land heavy.

Mikhail blinks once. Then again. He sits down abruptly, the leather chair creaking under his weight. "I'm sorry," he says. "Did I hear that right?"

"Yes."

He runs a hand through his hair, dislodging the careful calm he usually wears like armor. "You have a son? You're not mistaken?"

"I got a DNA test done," I inform him. "But I could tell even before that."

"So you had a child in Russia for a decade and none of us knew about it?" Mikhail stands up, looking agitated, stuffing his hands into his pockets. He's usually the calmest of my brothers, with the exception of Dmitry, who is a robot in human form.

"Yes."

"And the mother?" His voice is quieter now, cautious, like

he's afraid the answer might shatter something. "Who is the mother?"

"Who do you think? Anya, obviously."

He exhales sharply, staring at the desk. "You had a child in Russia," he says, incredulous, "and you never told us?"

"I didn't know, either," I reply. "I found out recently."

Mikhail lets out a short laugh that holds no humor. "? I used to think nothing escaped your attention."

"I was trying to forget about her. I proposed to her when we were younger. But she chose to marry Petrov. I was bitter. I wanted to pretend like she didn't exist." I have never been so forthcoming about my emotions, and Mikhail knows.

"You proposed to her? When?"

"A decade ago," I reply. "I was dating her after our parents died. Before that, too, but we broke up because our father didn't like her."

"So you started dating again after papa died?"

I nod. "She was a figure skater. World champion. I'm a gangster. It wasn't the usual match. She had money and a reputation to protect. So she chose a respectable man to marry in the end."

"But she had your kid? Without telling you?" Mikhail rubs his forehead, but the lines only deepen.

"She didn't tell Petrov, either. Petrov still believes Aleksandr is his son. And it's better that way."

"Better for whom?"

"For Aleksandr," I answer. "I'm a wanted man in Russia. He would suffer if people found out the truth."

Mikhail turns around, making an exasperated noise. I guess he knows he can't tell anyone about this. Especially not Dmitry and Nikolai. They're still young. And I'm not sure how Aleksei will react, either. Besides, if Anya and Aleksandr won't be part of my life anymore, then there's no reason for anybody to know about them.

"This will stay between us. Nobody must know I'm Aleksandr's father. Not even Zorina. Understood?"

Mikhail's eyebrows furrow. "I'm not lying to my wife."

"Fine. She can know. I daresay she might pick up something from Anya. But not our brothers. I don't trust Nikolai to keep his mouth shut."

Mikhail scratches his beard. "This sounds like a bad sitcom. A secret child for over a decade that you didn't know about. What are the chances?" He swallows. "So, what are you going to do now?"

"Help Anya get a divorce and get custody," I reply.

"Why is she getting a divorce now? Wasn't she happy with Petrov for so m any years? She picked him over you, Leo. So why are you making her leave him? If he thinks Aleksandr is his son, isn't that good?"

I consider whether to divulge more, but decide I've already come too far to back down. "He has been abusing them." I close my eyes, tipping my head backward. "There are scars on their bodies. I've seen them, and it haunts me at night. My son doesn't deserve to be treated that way. And neither does Anya."

Mikhail swears under his breath. "God, that's bad, then."

"Yes. I had to convince her to leave him, but she has made up her mind now. They're separated."

"And you're going to marry her after she's divorced?"

I grunt. "No. She'll live with her parents. They live in a small town. Nobody we know lives there. No gangs operate there. It's a safe place. The best I could expect."

"You don't want to live with your son?"

"I want to, but Anya is his mother. I will not separate them."

"Well, if you excuse me saying so, she seems very attracted to you. She might change her mind about marrying you."

I nod. "I hope she will. But I can't leave that to chance anymore. I lost enough time already. I won't lose more."

He finally takes a drink, then another. "So what are you planning?"

"I want to be in my son's life. And I want Anya as my wife. I want us to be a family." I pause. "Which is why I'm stepping down from the pakhan position. Temporarily. I need to focus on them."

His glass stops halfway to his mouth. "You're what? Are you crazy? You have been the leader of the organization for over a decade. People trust you. Who could replace you?"

"Dmitry will take over."

Mikhail sets the glass down hard. "Leo, that's drastic. Dmitry is still in college."

"He's good with logistics," I say evenly. "With patterns. With numbers. He understands the flow of money better than any of us. He's already running half our operations on paper. This won't be forever. A few months. Until the divorce is finalized. Until I know Anya and Aleksandr are safe."

"And then?" Mikhail asks.

"Then I come back. Whether or not she marries me."

He studies me. "If you love her, how can you let her go at all?"

"She's not ready for this world," I say. "And she's terrified our son will pay the price for my choices."

Mikhail leans back. "Zorina and I could keep the boy here. Las Vegas is safer. He would never be in danger."

"She'd never agree," I answer. "Anya won't be separated from him. Ever."

Silence settles between us, thick with old memories. Then Mikhail's eyes narrow.

"Petrov," he says slowly. "I knew the name rang a bell. I remember now."

I look up.

"It was after our parents died," he continues. "A year or two later. The St. Petersburg port seizures."

The room sharpens.

"He was behind it," Mikhail says. "Using the police. Anti-drug crackdowns. Making an example of cartels. We lost shipment after shipment. Cocaine, MDMA, everything. We were bleeding money."

"I remember," I say quietly. Too well.

Mikhail nods. "And then one day, one of your seized shipments was released. No explanation. Just...cleared."

My grip tightens around the glass.

"That was around the time Anya left me," I say. "And started seeing Petrov."

The pieces slide together with sick precision.

I stare at the amber liquid, seeing something else entirely. "I told her about the port. About the losses."

Mikhail's voice is careful now. "Do you think she—"

"No," I cut in. Then I hesitate. "I don't know."

But the timing claws at me.

I drain my glass.

Whatever the truth is, it's buried deep. And I intend to dig it out.

EIGHTEEN

Anya

FOURTEEN YEARS AGO...

THE SUN FINDS me even with my eyes closed.

Warmth presses into my skin, salt and citrus drifting on the breeze, the distant hush of waves folding over themselves again and again. I'm stretched out on a cushioned lounge chair, half dozing, half aware of the solid weight beside me. Leo's shoulder is close enough that our arms brush when I breathe in.

This doesn't feel real.

We're in Tulum, tucked away on a private stretch of beach that looks like it belongs in a travel magazine. Powder-soft sand. Palm trees leaning lazily toward turquoise water. No crowds, no whispers, no eyes that know who he is or what his name means in certain circles. Just sun, sea, and the sound of my heartbeat slowing for the first time in months.

I turn my face toward him. He's shirtless, sunglasses pushed into his hair, skin bronzed from days in the sun. He looks relaxed in a way I rarely see anymore. Less pakhan. More like my boyfriend. If anyone saw us now, they'd think we were just a normal couple.

I'm wearing my best bikini, my breasts spilling out. It hasn't slipped Leo's attention. He keeps adjusting the triangle cups of my bikini top any time I move, like he's worried I'm going to flash someone by accident.

Since we're on a private beach, there's no one. But his possessiveness till thrills me. I was afraid he'd be cold and distant and lose interest in me. We've been dating for almost two years since we got back together. Even though we've both been so busy, the phone calls have been frequent.

I admire the way Leo throws himself into the tough business of crime and entertainment. He's doing it all for his brothers, for his family. I never knew he was such a family man. I can't wait to someday become his family, too, to share the responsibilities he shoulders on the behalf of others.

"Are you asleep?" I murmur.

One corner of his mouth lifts. "I was. Until you started staring."

"I wasn't staring."

"You were thinking," he corrects. "That's worse."

I smile and prop myself up on one elbow. "It feels like a fantasy. You, me, a beach, no danger. No walls."

"It does feel like a dream," he says calmly. There's a wistful note in his voice. He's so used to being in danger, to looking over his shoulder, to carrying a gun, that I had to forbid him from bringing one to the beach. I mean, where exactly would he hide it in his swim trunks. The other guests at the hotel would just stare at us. "No one cares who I am here. There are no enemies. No biting cold, either. Just you and me."

"And yet you're still working," I tease. "The only reason we're here is because you're trying to make a business deal with the cartels around here."

He exhales, amused. "Some habits don't disappear just because the view improves."

"But I'm glad you took me along for your business trip." I trace patterns on his chest with my fingertips. There's dark hair matting the broad, muscular plane of his chest. When I lay my ear against him, I can hear his heartbeat. It's slow and sensual, when it's usually fast and skittish.

This vacation is doing him a world of good. Even his dark circles look better. His complexion has improved, thanks to tanning in the sun.

Something tugs in my chest. How I wish we could live here forever, as nothing more than carefree lovers.

He reaches out, resting his hand on my stomach, his thumb moving in a slow, absent circle against my skin. I feel my pussy clench as his fingers dip downward, but I know he won't try anything while we're in a public place. He's too jealous to let other men see me naked.

"It's been a busy year," I say quietly. "I feel like I've lived three lifetimes."

"So have I," he replies. "Only mine involved less applause."

"I'm building something bigger," he continues. "In the US and Russia. I don't want everything tied to one place. Russia is... unpredictable. Corruption won't disappear. It never does. I want to protect my brothers. I want to keep them in America, away from Kremlin politics. Away from the danger and crime. I want them to have freedom, to live the life I couldn't love. My dad had a few legal businesses in the United States, mostly to launder money. But now we're expanding our legal business portfolio. Instead of using them for laundering money, I'll use them to make money and fund the drug business. We've been losing shipments of cocaine recently. Those losses add up over time."

I take his hand, brushing my thumb across his knuckles. "You'd make a great dad."

Leo quirks a thick, brown eyebrow immediately. "Where did that come from?"

"What do you mean where? Seeing you act like a patriarch, thinking about your family's future, pushing yourself, never sleeping, never slowing down, just so they can have the life you never did. That's very fatherly, you know."

"Is that what your father was like?" Leo blinks at me, curious.

"Well, maybe. He worked hard, but he only had an ordinary job. He and my mother made sacrifices so they could save enough money to send me to Moscow." I poke Leo's cheek. "But he didn't have half as many lines as you do. And you're so much younger than him."

"Work ages you." Leo grunts when I pinch the lines on his forehead. "Stop doing that."

"You're going to become an old man before you ever have kids."

"It doesn't matter." Leo shrugs. "All that matters is if I can keep them safe and give them a good life. I'm going to make money and create a legacy they can rely on so they never have to work if they don't want to."

He swallows, looking at me with tenderness. This is something else that has changed about him. I always knew he loved me, and he showed it with his actions and words. Now he shows it with his vulnerable, unguarded expression, too. He's a big, scary gangster most of the time. So I feel special that I'm the only one who knows how truly kind and caring he can be.

I glance at him. "You talk to me about it now. Your future

plans. Your work. And I like hearing about it. Building a secondary empire in America is a cool idea."

He cups one side of my face. "Because I trust you."

The word settles into me, warm and steady. "As you should. I'm your girlfriend."

"Enough about me. What about you? Are you looking forward to skating on the ice once we go back?"

I trace patterns on the back of his hand. "My season's been good. Not perfect, but good. I won in Paris. Took silver in Stockholm. Lost in Milan, which still annoys me."

His mouth curves. "You hate losing."

"I hate losing when I know I could have done better." I pause. "Winning Worlds again feels... daunting. Like tempting fate."

"You thrive on daunting," he says. "You always have."

"I think being with you makes me more ambitious," I admit. "You never stop. You never settle. It makes me want to push harder, too."

He studies me, something tender flickering behind his eyes.

"I'm glad we're dating again," I say softly. "Time flies when I'm with you."

He leans in, pressing a kiss to my temple. "It does."

I hesitate, then ask, "I can't wait to meet your brothers. You said they'd be in Russia when we return."

His body stills, just slightly.

"Not yet," he says after a beat. "Dmitry and Nikolai are still young. It's... complicated. I don't think you should meet them yet."

I nod, though disappointment tugs at me. "I promised you I'd retire after two years. That time is almost up." I meet his gaze. "I'm ready to marry you, Leo."

His hand slides up to my shoulder, thumb brushing gently. "Are you sure?"

"Yes." No hesitation. "If I win Worlds again, it'll be the perfect goodbye. I'll be thirty soon. It feels like the right moment."

He exhales slowly. "I'll come watch you skate this time."

My face lights up. "Really?"

"Yes."

"You're the best boyfriend," I say, laughing.

He smiles, but there's a faint tension there, a shadow that wasn't present before. Not fear. Responsibility.

I lean forward, wrapping my arms around him. He holds me close, solid and warm, like an anchor.

"Enough talking," I say suddenly. "We're on vacation."

I grab his hand and tug. "Come on."

"Anya—"

Too late.

I pull him toward the water, laughing as waves lap at our legs. I splash him. He retaliates immediately, lifting me off my feet and dumping us both into the sea. I shriek, then laugh so hard my chest aches.

We float, tangled and breathless, sunlight dancing over the surface.

I look at him and think, *This is it.*

This happiness.

I can't wait to have this forever.

ONE YEAR LATER....

THE COLD BITES straight through my bones.

I wrap my fur coat tighter around myself as I climb the steps to Leo's townhouse, my breath coming out in white clouds that vanish as quickly as his promises have lately. Moscow winters have always been cruel, but tonight they feel personal. Like the city itself is punishing me for hoping.

He hasn't called in weeks.

Not once since he told me, in a clipped, distracted voice, that several cocaine shipments had been seized. Not once since the police pressure started tightening. Even before that, there were cracks. Missed calls. Cancelled plans. Excuses that sounded rehearsed.

And then he broke his promise to me.

The World Championships final was here in Moscow. My home ice. I told everyone my boyfriend would be there. I searched the stands anyway, even when I knew better. I skated like my heart was splitting open, like maybe if I won hard enough, he'd feel it wherever he was.

But Leo never came. It was so close, and he was in the same city, but he couldn't be bothered to come and watch me. I didn't try to hold it against him. He had told me he couldn't talk to me much because he was busy. But his absence really hurt me. It's like I don't matter to him at all. He couldn't even make an hour for me. I have been patient for months, trying to be understanding when he stopped calling, when he stopped coming around. I'd go to his house like an eager puppy, and every time I was told he wasn't at home, I would come back, disappointed.

The door to his house looks like it belongs it a palace. It has a brass door knocked, and two lion statues on either side, true to Leo's name.

The guards at the entrance straighten when they see me.

"I'm Anya Vasilieva," I say, my voice sharper than I intend.

They exchange a glance, then step aside. "Of course."

Inside, the house is silent. Vast. Beautiful. Empty.

Crystal chandeliers. Marble floors. Art that costs more than my childhood home. The place smells faintly of leather and expensive cologne. It has never felt less like somewhere people live.

The housekeeper looks up from the hallway and smiles kindly. "Dobry vecher, Anya."

I force a nod. "Dobry vecher."

I've slept in Leo's bed. Eaten dinners she cooked for us. Walked these halls barefoot at dawn while he watched me like I was something precious.

Tonight, the walls feel like they're closing in.

I don't knock.

I push open the door to his study.

He's behind the desk, sleeves rolled up, jacket discarded, phone pressed to his ear. Papers are scattered everywhere. His laptop glows harshly in the dim light. He looks... different. Broader, heavier through the shoulders. His face is gaunter, eyes sunken, shadows carved deep beneath them. The boy who once smiled at me on an ice rink feels like a lifetime ago.

He finishes the call without looking at me.

"Move the shipment through Odessa," he says coldly. "I don't care how much it costs."

The line goes dead.

I stand there, shaking.

"Are you avoiding me?" I ask.

He doesn't look up. "Don't be childish."

The word lands like a slap.

"I've called you," I say. "I've left messages. You haven't answered once."

"I'm busy." His fingers move across the keyboard. "You know that."

Busy.

Not too busy to promise he'd come to my competition. Not too busy to tell me, months ago, that I was his future.

"You didn't come," I say quietly. "You said you would."

Silence.

He exhales through his nose, irritated. "Things came up."

"Things always come up," I snap. "But I was there. On the ice. Looking for you."

He finally looks at me then, and his gaze is distant. Impatient.

"You lost," he says flatly. "What difference would it have made?"

The words knock the air out of my chest.

I stare at him. "You don't mean that."

"I don't have time for this," he says, rubbing his temples. "My entire operation is under pressure. I'm fighting the police, rivals, politicians. And you want to talk about an insignificant competition right now. Give me a break, Anya."

He has never talked like this to me before. Even when he was sarcastic and grumpy, he was never condescending. He never treated me like I was an immature girl who was an nuisance to him.

Anger rattles in my bones. I take a deep breath, trying to quench the trail of fire burning my insides. I want to shake him awake, tell him he can't treat me like this. Can't shut me out when it's convenient.

I slam my hand down on the desk. Hard. The sound echoes.

"You didn't even answer my calls," I say, my voice breaking. "I forgave you for missing the competition. I forgave everything. But you couldn't even pick up the phone or congratulate me for making it to the finals. I was crying when I lost. I needed you. I needed to hear your voice."

My voice breaks, revealing the emotions I have bottled up for weeks. Leo has always been my rock, my comfort. He was always by my side when I needed him.

"You're an adult now, Anya. You can't expect comfort like a child." He stands abruptly. "You should be independent."

My nails scrape against the wooden surface of his table. His words are like knives, stabbing me in the softest places.

"I didn't just call for comfort," I say, sniffling. It's inevitable now—I'm going to cry. Leo Antonov is breaking my heart and he doesn't even know it. I wonder if he cares. "I wanted to ask you about how things were with your work, too."

"You think my life stops because you want reassurance?" he continues, his tone sharp, cutting. "I'm not a skater who can cry and try again next season. People die when I make mistakes."

"I never asked you to stop," I say, tears burning my eyes. "I asked you to care."

His jaw tightens. "You knew what you were getting into."

No.

I knew the man who held my hand at the rink. Who believed in me when I didn't believe in myself. Not this stranger who looks at me like I'm an inconvenience.

"Are you lashing out at me because of work? Because that is not okay." I raise my volume. I want him to take me seriously, but he's not even seeing me or my emotions anymore. It's like he has stopped caring about us.

"The authorities and politicians in St. Petersburg have it out for me."

"Maybe I can help," I say. "Is there anyone I can talk to?"

Leo's mouth flattens. "No. I will handle it. I don't need your help, malishka. You're just a woman. You shouldn't get involved in this."

"So what if I'm a woman? I'm a powerful one. I have sponsors, many of whom are in the government." I hesitate, wondering whether I should tell him about the guy named Petrov who hugged me when I cried after losing the finals. He said I deserved to win, and invited me to have coffee with him. I knew he was trying to get with me romantically, so I said I had a boyfriend. He said to call him if anything changes. He was classy and well-mannered, a real upper-class gentleman. I was charmed by him, but of course, I love Leo. I wonder if Leo will snap out of it when I tell him someone else wants me. If I can't make him care, I'll make him jealous. "There's a guy who is interested in me, too. A politician. He gave me roses. I could ask him."

Leo scoffs. "It must feel good. They're trying to tear me down, but they're desperate to support a girl who parades around on the ice."

I swallow, but my rage cannot be contained. Leo never let on that he saw me in such an unflattering light. Fear makes my stomach clench. What if he has resented me all along? Like other men, maybe he thinks I have it easy because I do something fun. "I figure skate. That's an Olympic sport," I say. "If you don't like it, then why did you ever date me?"

He sighs. "Anya, don't throw a tantrum. You know I didn't mean it like that."

I freeze.

Leo has never raised his voice at me before.

"I don't even know you anymore," I whisper. My eyes sting. I can feel the pressure building up, but I don't want to cry in front of Leo. I no longer feel safe doing that. The way he is now, he'll accuse me of using my womanly wiles.

He turns back to his desk. "Then leave."

The dismissal is casual. Cruel.

I swallow hard. "Alright. But if I do, we're breaking up."

He doesn't turn around.

"Fine," he says. "If that means you'll leave. I need to work."

That's it.

That's all I'm worth.

My vision blurs. "You're empty," I say, my voice shaking. "You've forgotten how to be human. You're just... an empire now."

His shoulders tense, but he doesn't respond.

I walk out before I completely shatter.

The cold hits me like punishment as I step back into the night. Snow crunches beneath my boots. Tears spill freely now, freezing on my lashes.

I loved him. I still do. But love isn't enough when someone stops seeing you. When they're so consumed by their fear and obsession that everything else ceases to matter.

I disappear into the winter, my sobs swallowed by the city that taught me how to endure—and how to let go.

NINETEEN

Leo

ANYA IS on top of me when I wake.

Not beside me. On me. Straddling my hips, naked, her hair loose and wild around her shoulders. Morning light spills through the tall windows, turning her skin to gold. Her breasts are heavy and full, nipples already tight. Her hips are wide and perfect, the soft curve of her stomach leading down to where she's wet and ready.

"Aleksandr is still asleep," she whispers, her voice husky. Her hand wraps around my cock, stroking slowly. "And you're so hard, Leo. Let me take care of you with my pussy."

I'm fully awake now, every nerve ending firing. Her golden hair spills down her shoulders. I can't resist reaching up with my fingers, tangling them in the silky softness of her tresses. I usually wake up to phone calls and bad news. But this morning is beautiful. I get to wake up to a sexy mommy giving me what I need to make my day better. "Anya—"

She positions herself over me, the head of my cock brushing against her entrance. "I want to feel you inside me. Bare. No barriers."

"No barriers?" I smile. "You want me to breed you. You're such a cum slut."

She throws me a saucy look. "I like feeling the texture of your veins and your skin inside me. It makes the experience a million times better."

I narrow my eyes as the light coming in from the windows gets brighter. I can hear sounds below, sounds of violin. Zorina must already be awake and practicing. The beautiful serenade she's playing is the perfect soundtrack for early morning sex.

"You look like a MILF trying to seduce an innocent boy," I groan as she grinds herself against me, smearing her pussy juices all over my aching cock. I grip her hips, smacking her ass. "You look like every fantasy I've ever had."

"I can't wait anymore. I'm going to take you inside me." Anya blinks. When I nod, she sinks down slowly. An exquisite pleasure lights up my body when the head of my cock pushes against her tight entrance. When she swallows the first inch, heat erupts in my groin. That fire keeps growing, blazing into an inferno, making me feel like I'm being charred from the inside with every inch she takes.

Her pussy stretches beautifully, and yet it also squeezes around my hard shaft, milking me for every bit of pleasure. Each convulse triggers an electric bolt through me.

My spine tingles when my cock rubs against her insides.

She sinks down slowly, breasts bouncing as she moves. The feeling of her bare pussy gripping my cock makes my eyes roll back. Hot. Tight. Perfect.

"Fuck," I breathe. "How can you look so respectable on the outside and take cock so well when you're with me?"

Anya starts to move, rolling her hips, riding me with practiced ease. I watch her breasts bounce with each movement, watch where my thick cock disappears inside her. The slight pressure of her ass cheeks against my balls every time she takes me fully sends a zap of electric current straight to my brain.

The sensations envelop me. I feel like I'm drowning with every thrust. The pleasure builds up fast, friction brushing against my veiny cock every time it pushes into her channel. Anya starts to move faster.

"That's it," I growl. "Ride my cock like the greedy cum slut you are."

She moans, her head falling back, exposing the long line of her throat. I reach up, cupping her breasts, squeezing them roughly. They overflow my hands, soft and warm. I tease her hard peaks, making her cry.

"You like that?" I ask, pinching her nipples. "You like riding my bare cock?"

"Yes," she gasps. "I love it."

I move one hand down between her legs, finding her clit. It's swollen and sensitive, and when I rub it, she clenches around me.

"I could knock you up right now," I tell her, my voice rough. "Fill you so full of cum you'd have no choice but to carry my baby in your belly. Give Aleksandr a little brother or sister."

She laughs breathlessly. "I'm over forty, Leo. That won't happen so easily."

Maybe not. But the forbidden thrill of it—of feeling her naked, unprotected, her velvet walls clenching around me—makes my blood run hot. She feels like home.

I thrust up into her, meeting her movements, going deeper. Each stroke hits that spot that makes her cry out. I can feel her cervix, can feel how deep I am.

It takes every bit of self-control to keep myself from surrendering to my release. Her pussy seduces me, clenching rhythmically, making me want to give up and just cream her.

"Touch yourself," I command. "I want to feel you come on my cock."

She obeys, her fingers joining mine on her clit. The dual sensation makes her movements frantic, desperate. Her pussy is dripping, coating both of us.

"Leo," she gasps. "I'm close."

"Then come," I growl, pinching her clit hard.

She shatters, her orgasm ripping through her. Her pussy clamps down on me rhythmically, milking me, and I can't hold back. I thrust up hard, burying myself as deep as possible, and come with a groan. Hot spurts fill her, painting her insides, claiming her.

"Take it all," I mutter, my hands crushing her breasts as she continues to ride me through both our orgasms. "Every drop. You like when your pussy is filled with cum, don't you? That's why you keep begging me to take you bare."

"Yes, I love it," Anya admits. "But only when it's your cum."

She collapses forward onto my chest, both of us breathing hard. I stroke her back, feeling the sweat cooling on her skin. Her breasts feel pleasantly plump against my chest.

"I'm taking you and Aleksandr out today," I say after a moment. "To an amusement park."

She lifts her head, her eyes softening. "You love to spoil us."

"That's because you're both mine to spoil," I reply simply.

THE AMUSEMENT PARK smells like sugar and oil and damp winter air.

It is loud in a way that has nothing to do with danger. Children shriek. Music blares out of tinny speakers. Somewhere, a machine clanks and whirs like it is about to fall apart, and people line up anyway, smiling.

Aleksandr's hand is warm in mine. He keeps craning his neck to look at everything at once, eyes wide, taking it all in like he is afraid it might vanish if he blinks.

Anya walks on my other side, her coat brushing my arm. She looks lighter today. Not carefree, but softer. Less guarded.

"You sure this was the right thing to do?" she says quietly as Aleksandr pulls me toward a stand selling balloons shaped like animals. "If you start getting attached to him now, it'll be hard to let go later."

"I know," I reply. "But I need to know that I did my best for my son. That I gave him a chance to get to know his father and spend time with him."

She exhales. "When the divorce is final, and he moves away from you... it might hurt. I don't want you to feel like you lost something."

I look down at the boy tugging on my sleeve. "I already lost too much," I say. "If I get hurt later, I'll live with it. I don't want regrets."

I stare at the clouds shifting overhead. I'm feeling both emotional and philosophical today. When my head cleared after the orgasm and we went downstairs for dinner, looking at Aleksandr in his pajamas made a strange ache erupt in my chest. He looked so innocent, so young and untainted, that for a second, I wondered what he was doing in my house.

I want him to always be that way. To only talk about guns as a fun and forbidden subjects, not a daily reality of life. I want him to think of balloons and theme parks, Disneyland and Lego, not money laundering and ingenious ways of hiding shipments in containers.

My younger brothers Dmitry and Nikolai were both raised

with a constant stream of soldiers coming in and out of the house. Dmitry developed an interest in computers, hacking, and using both to launder money in his tweens. He was already a pro by the time he went to college. Nikolai learned charm and psychological manipulation without even trying to. I'm proud of the men they have both become. They're reliable, trustworthy, and they're both growing their own families while shouldering burdens in the organization. But things could have been so different for them. Dmitry could have been a tech genius with international acclaim if he had applied his genius elsewhere. Nikolai could have been a movie star, giving joy to people. Well, I pushed him to be a politician, so he might yet do some good for society.

My thoughts scatter when Aleksandr tugs on my coat.

"Can we ride that?"

He is pointing at a carousel. Painted horses bob up and down under blinking lights.

Anya laughs. "Of course you want the horses."

I arch a brow. "I am not getting on a horse."

Aleksandr grins. "You have to. You're big. It will be funny."

Anya covers her mouth, already laughing.

Five minutes later, I am sitting on a white carousel horse that is clearly not designed for a man my size. My knees are nearly at my chest. The pole creaks ominously. Even when I was a kid, I never did things like this. My father never encouraged me to have fun or took me to an amusement park, only to seedy pubs and bowling alleys where money and drugs were exchanged. I feel some pride at being a better father. I might have to tell Mikhail when I go back that someday, when his son is old enough, he should bring him here, too.

Aleksandr is on the horse beside me, beaming. The horses aren't moving fast, but there's a breeze that brushes the brown locks of his hair into his eyes. I reach over and brush them away.

It feels like a paternal thing to do, and even Aleksandr's eyes widen.

"You look ridiculous," Anya calls out, taking pictures of us from the side, barely hiding her laughter. I like seeing her happy, even if it's coming at the cost of my pride.

"I am dignified," I say flatly.

The ride starts. The horse rises and falls. Children laugh. Music plays. It feels surreal for a moment, like I've been thrown back in time. I feel like a kid again, holding Aleksandr's hand, riding a carousel horse for the first time. It's more fun than I imagined. There's something magical about it.

Aleksandr leans toward me. "You don't look like a gangster right now."

"Then what do I look like?"

"A prince from a fairytale. You're riding a white horse." Aleksandr looks me straight in the eye. "Zorina told me that in the past, heroes and knights used to ride on a white horse and save people. You rode in a black Mercedes, but you saved me and mama."

My throat clenches. Emotions tremble in my chest, but they're too new for me to comprehend.

"You don't make any sense. And heroes ride real horses, not plastic ones."

Aleksandr giggles. "Can you ride a real horse?"

"No. But one of my brothers can. His name is Nikolai. He studied at a boarding school in England."

"Do they teach you to ride horses in England."

"If you pay them enough, they do."

"Can I go to England, too, and learn to ride horses?"

I scoff. "I thought you wanted guns."

"I want both. I'll shoot my gun while riding a horse. Doesn't that sound cool?"

I open my mouth, then close it. I was going to promise to

take him to England, to get him a horse-riding instructor. It would be easy. We could take my private jet there every weekend. London isn't far from Moscow. He could get lessons. But he'd have to stop when Anya's divorce comes through. And I'm not sure he deserves the disappointment.

"You can learn to ride horses in Russia, too. Ask you mama to get you lessons," I say.

Aleksandr sighs. "She won't. She says it's dangerous to go out of the house."

"Maybe she's right," I say.

He deflates.

After the carousel, there are bumper cars. Aleksandr insists we all go together.

Anya squeals when I ram into her car on purpose.

"Leo," she scolds, laughing. "You're cheating."

"There are no rules," I say.

Aleksandr whoops as he crashes into both of us. "I win."

"You absolutely do not," I tell him. "I let you."

He looks at me with a seriousness that feels too old for his face. "That's what grown-ups always say."

We eat hot dogs standing up, mustard dripping onto napkins. Aleksandr gets ice cream after, vanilla with chocolate sauce. It melts faster than he can eat it.

Anya wipes his chin. "Slow down."

He shakes his head. "It's going to disappear."

I watch them. The way she touches him without thinking. The way he leans into her like it is the safest place in the world.

Something tightens in my chest.

As the sun sinks, lights flicker on all around us. The Ferris wheel glows against the darkening sky.

"Have you been on a Ferris wheel before?" I ask him. I've never been on one, and I've always wanted to go. Being with a kid is making me realize how many of my own desires as a kid I never got to fulfill.

"No, is it fast?" he asks, scared.

"It barely moves," I reply. "And when we're at the top, we can see the entire city."

"Will it be scary when we're up high?" His lips tremble.

"No, I'll hold your hand." I close my fingers around his, taking his hand. "Did you forget, I'm the strongest and most powerful man in Russia?"

He looks up at me, eyes glittering with trust and admiration. "You are."

Anya hesitates, smoothing a hand over Aleksandr's hair. "Are you sure? You can't come back down once we're up."

"I am not afraid," he says promptly. "Mr. Leo will protect me."

I hide a smile. "That's right."

The gondola sways as we climb in. Aleksandr sits between us, legs swinging. The wheel begins to turn, lifting us higher, the park shrinking below.

The city lights spread out in the distance, a sea of gold and white. The buildings spread out like paints on a canvas.

Aleksandr presses his face to the glass. "It looks like stars. So many lights."

Anya leans back, her shoulder brushing mine. "It is beautiful. I will remember this forever."

I nod. "So will I."

At the top, the wheel slows. The world feels suspended. I cling to Aleksandr's hand, keeping my grip firm but not too tight. He seems to have forgotten all about his fears and is immersed in the view.

Anya looks at me from the opposite seat, as if she knows what I'm thinking.

"I didn't know this," I admit quietly. "What it feels like."

Anya looks at me. "A family?"

"Yes."

She reaches for my hand, threading her fingers through mine. "I told you. You will miss it."

I squeeze her hand once. I already know she is right.

The wheel begins to descend, and I hold on to the moment as tightly as I can, knowing some things are borrowed, even when they feel like they should be forever.

TWENTY

Anya

TWELVE YEARS AGO...

THE RING IS HEAVY.

It sits on my finger like a promise I didn't quite understand when I made it, the diamond catching the chandelier light and scattering it back at the room in obedient flashes. It's an heirloom, Petrov told me proudly. Old money. Old power. The kind of ring women whisper about.

They do whisper about it.

"Oh, my dear, that stone is extraordinary."

"You're such a lucky woman."

"He must adore you."

I smile. I nod. I let them turn my hand this way and that, admire the cut, the clarity, the weight of it. I say thank you like a well-trained doll.

I don't feel lucky.

I'm attending yet another fundraiser today for my fiancé's political campaign. He is keen to get voted again. He has been on edge the last few weeks, trying to schmooze with bigwigs to make sure he wins this time.

The fundraiser is held in a restored mansion near the river, all polished marble and velvet drapes, the air thick with perfume and ambition. Men in tailored suits cluster in tight circles, murmuring about policy and ports and money. Women stand beside them like punctuation marks, decorative and quiet.

Petrov's hand rests at the small of my back, possessive but distracted. His attention keeps drifting, his eyes lingering too long on a woman in a silver dress across the room. She laughs at something he says from a distance, her hand brushing his arm.

I pretend not to notice.

I've learned how to do that.

"You're doing wonderfully," Petrov murmurs, leaning down to my ear. "Everyone loves you."

I glance up at him. He looks impeccable. Blond hair perfectly styled, smile polished for public consumption. Respectable. Powerful. Safe.

"Do they?" I ask softly.

"Of course. You're a famous figure skater. They're all curious about how I got someone like you to marry me." He straightens my posture with a subtle pressure of his hand. "Smile."

I don't hesitate to obey. I know keeping him happy is my best bet at a secure future. Even though I have an apartment I bought with my prize money and some savings in the bank, it's not enough to sustain me long-term. I don't know what other job I could do. Even if I did, being Petrov's wife feels like the safest option.

After my breakup with Leo, I haven't been able to feel anything. I'm apathetic. I just don't care anymore. When he coldly rejected me, it broke something inside me. My ability to feel and care is gone. Now I only make practical decisions, because being emotional and choosing a gangster twice led to nothing but heartbreak.

I tell myself Petrov is the kind of man most women dream of. He's a gentleman with impeccable polish and manners. He doesn't have living parents, and that means I don't have to deal with problems from my in-laws. I try to focus on the positives.

Anything to avoid facing the truth: I'm not really attracted to Petrov. Not anymore.

His charm started to wear off a few months later. By then, it was too late. I was in too deep. I had asked him to return Leo's shipments that were seized at the St. Petersburg port and to let new ones come in. A favor like that would cost me. I knew it back then, but I wanted to ease Leo's burden. We had already broken up, but the haunted and troubled expression he wore when I went to his study stuck with me.

I started dating Petrov right after. It was a rebound. He was so eager and affectionate, taking me out to dates and public parties. When I brought up the issue with Leo, he didn't seem fazed. I didn't tell him I'd been dating Leo, just that my parents owed him something. Petrov must have thought Leo would threaten them, so he released the shipments.

Now, as his puts his arm around my waist, I feel less like his girlfriend and more like a trophy wife. He takes me to all his political events, where I'm expected to wear conservative clothes, smile, and say the right things. I quit figure skating after I broke up with Leo. I didn't have it in me to continue after that crushing defeat in the World Championships.

We move through the room, stopping every few steps so he can shake hands, accept donations, exchange pleasantries.

"This is my fiancée," he says again and again. "Anya."

They recognize me. The former figure skater. The golden girl who retired too early.

"You were magnificent on the ice," a man tells me. "Such grace."

"Thank you," I reply automatically.

I don't tell him that I quit because my heart broke and never quite put itself back together.

"Are you tired?" Petrov asks, noticing my silence.

"I'm fine," I lie.

He squeezes my waist. "Good. We still need to speak to Volkov."

We approach another group. More smiles. More empty words.

I listen to Petrov talk about reform and infrastructure while my mind drifts. I think about quiet mornings. About ice under my blades. About a man who used to look at me like I was the only thing in the world worth seeing.

Petrov laughs at something someone says. I laugh a beat too late.

Maybe this is enough, I tell myself. He isn't cruel. He doesn't shout. He doesn't disappear without explanation. My parents approve of him. My life will be comfortable. I won't have to look over my shoulder anymore.

There is no danger here. No bullets. No threats. No secrecy. But also no passion, no heat, no emotional comfort, no multiple orgasms and sex that makes my toes curl.

I inhale, and it feels like the air smells different now. I look up. Then the room shifts.

It's subtle. A change in the air. The way my chest tightens before I even understand why.

I look up.

And there he is.

Leo stands near the bar, a glass in his hand, dark suit molded to his broad frame. His hair is combed back now. He looks sharper. There's a polish about him that suggests he has learned to adapt to the world of politics and business. He doesn't look like a thug anymore. In fact, if he introduced himself as a businessman, I would never question it.

When his eyes meet mine, everything else disappears. There's so much pain in those eyes. Or is it my own loneliness that I see reflected in the gray?

His lips part slightly, and I watch him mouth my name. Anya.

The noise fades. The lights blur. The world spins like it is ending.

He looks at me like he's seen a ghost.

I look at him like I've been haunted for years.

He looks better. Stronger. More powerful. And still unbearably familiar.

My heart stutters.

I realize, with terrifying clarity, that I never stopped loving him. Not for a second. And now that he's in front of me, my heart feels like it's being violently torn from the inside.

He inhales, waiting for me to react. Petrov finished talking to Volkov. He looks around, as if trying to find someone else he can pester for a donation.

I slide my arm away from his. "Honey, can I go to the bathroom? I'll be back soon."

"Of course. I should have thought of it." His words are polite and considerate, but his gaze is fixed on the woman in the silver dress. I realize he wants me gone for a different reason. Still, I trust him. I know he often looks at beautiful women at a party, but nothing ever comes out of it. He cares about his image, especially now that the elections are close. He won't destroy it by cheating on me.

My heels punch against the floor, making sharp sounds that are swallowed up by the conversations buzzing around me. I track through the floor, past Leo, out of the venue room toward the bathrooms.

The sounds follow me. I know they're his footsteps. They're both silent and heavy, sure yet soft.

Leo is following me. But why? Does he have anything left to say to me? Does he want to apologize? But it's too late now. I'm somebody else's fiancée.

My pulse jumps, sharp and disobedient, as I move faster down the corridor. The chatter from the main hall fades, replaced by muted music and the hush of velvet-lined walls. I push past a corner, then another, until the light thins and the hallway narrows into something quieter. More private.

I stop.

I don't know why I do it. Maybe because running has never really worked for me. Maybe because some part of me has been waiting months for this moment.

His steps stop behind me.

I don't turn right away. My hands are clenched so tightly at my sides that my fingers ache.

"Anya," he says.

Just my name. Nothing else.

I face him.

He steps out of the shadows, and suddenly he's too close. Close enough that I can smell his cologne. Close enough that the memory of his hands, his mouth, his weight crashes into me without mercy.

My body heats from the inside, finally feeling alive. And all he had to do was breathe next to me. My body is a traitor.

For a second, neither of us speaks.

"How have you been?" he asks finally.

The question is simple. Ordinary. It devastates me anyway.

Because being asked that by Leo used to be the highlight of my days. He used to always ask me how I was, every time he called me. Before my competitions. And I realize, bitterly, that for all his politeness, Petrov never asks me how I'm doing.

"I'm fine," I say, the words heavy on my tongue. "Busy. I have a wedding to plan." I lift my chin. "And you? How's work?"

We're not old friends. We're old lovers. And the tinge if disappointment is a heavy weight between us.

His mouth twitches, humorless. "Better. Much better."

Of course it is. Everything always improves once I'm no longer in his life.

Silence stretches, thick and brittle. There are so many things pressing against my ribs that I don't know which one will escape first.

He exhales, slow and controlled, like he's bracing himself. "I missed you."

The words land softly. They still knock the air from my lungs.

"I shouldn't say that," he adds. "But I did. I do."

I swallow. "Leo—"

"I treated you carelessly," he continues, voice lower now, stripped of its usual steel. "I know that. I spent nights replaying that day. Wondering why I didn't stop you. Why I let you walk out like you meant nothing."

My chest burns.

"I wanted to come after you," he says. "I should have. But then I heard you were seeing Petrov."

My jaw tightens. "We're engaged."

The word feels strange in my mouth. Heavy. Final.

He doesn't congratulate me.

Instead, he looks at me like I've wounded him. "Then I need to say this now," he says. "I want to marry you."

The world tilts.

"What?" I whisper.

"You're not married yet," he says quickly. "An engagement can be broken. Come with me. Be my wife. Let's create the family we always dreamed of."

My heart is pounding so hard it hurts. "I chose Petrov. I'm not a woman who betrays my man."

"You chose safety," he counters. "That's not the same thing."

"Being with someone whose life isn't constantly in danger feels good," I snap. "I'm respected. I'm welcomed. He's everything I should have loved from the start."

"But you don't love him."

The certainty in his voice makes my temper flare. "You don't know that."

"I do," he says quietly. "You never smile for him the way you smiled for me. You stiffen when he touches you. You look bored. Like you're waiting for the night to end."

"That's the nature of fundraising events," I retort.

"You don't have to lie to me," he says. "You never could."

And that's the cruelest part. He's right. He always saw me too clearly. Not just my victories, but my doubts. My unhappiness before I admitted it to myself.

"I'm allowed to marry for practical reasons," I say, my voice shaking. "Love isn't everything."

"You're not built for practicality, Anya," he says. "I have known you for years. You're a dreamer. You live passionately. You pursue what your heart desires, and never settle for less. That's why I was drawn to you. A cold marriage will kill you slowly."

The truth of it lodges painfully in my chest.

But so does my pride.

"You hurt me," I say. "You threw me away when I needed

you. You decided I was expendable." My eyes sting. "And now you want me because it's convenient."

His face tightens. "That's not—"

"I have self-respect," I continue. "I won't be someone you pick up again when you're ready."

He reaches for my hand. His fingers are warm. Familiar.

"My offer stands," he says softly. "Until the day you marry him. If you change your mind, my door is open."

I yank my hand free.

"I will never come back to you," I say, furious and wounded and terrified by how much this hurts. "No matter what."

For a moment, he looks like he might argue. Then he nods once, sharply, as if sealing something shut inside himself. "I love you, Anya. I will move heaven and earth for you if you marry me."

I turn and walk away before I break.

Behind me, the shadows swallow him again.

TWENTY-ONE

Leo

"I MADE HIM JUMP!" Aleksandr yells, waving at me with one gloved hand as his pony prances in a neat, awkward arc over a low wooden pole.

I straighten from where I'm leaning against the fence. "I saw," I call back. "Don't let him think he's smarter than you."

The instructor laughs softly beside him, a middle-aged woman in a padded jacket and riding boots, patient and firm in the way people are when they're used to children and animals. The pony, a stocky chestnut with a cropped mane, snorts like it's offended by the whole affair.

Aleksandr grins, teeth flashing. He sits straighter in the saddle, pride written all over his small, serious face.

This place is about forty minutes outside Moscow, tucked behind a line of bare birch trees and a low wooden gate that creaks when you push it open. A private riding school. Not flashy. No banners or sponsors. Just a wide indoor arena, the smell of hay and leather, and children learning how to balance on something bigger than themselves.

I didn't plan this.

It started as curiosity. Then routine. Then something I didn't want to name.

Anya still thinks I babysit him. She leaves him with me every Saturday when she goes to see her aunt and uncle, trusting me without knowing what I do with that trust. I tell myself I'm not lying. I'm just... omitting.

"Again?" Aleksandr asks eagerly as the pony circles back.

The instructor looks at me. "One more jump. Then we cool him down."

I nod. "One more."

Aleksandr urges the pony forward, heels clumsy, hands too tight on the reins. He clears the pole again, cleaner this time.

"Yes!" he shouts.

I clap once, sharp and loud. The sound surprises even me.

He beams.

Something in my chest loosens.

It has been more than two months since Las Vegas. Since I rode a carousel horse with my son and he begged me for riding lessons. I knew Anya would object. Especially if she knew I was the one taking him. Being seen with him can be bad, but this place is in the middle of nowhere, and nobody I know would come here.

Besides, I'm no longer the pakhan. It's now Dmitry's responsibility. I still handle some administrative affairs and the bigger deals which require authority, but Dmitry does most of the work. It's his face people see.

After the lessons, Aleksandr dismounts carefully, boots thudding against the packed dirt. He runs over, cheeks flushed, hair sticking out from under his helmet.

"Did you see how high he jumped?" he asks, breathless.

"I did," I say. "You're getting better."

He nods, satisfied. "Next time, I want to jump higher."

"Of course you do."

We've fallen into a rhythm.

After his riding lessons, we get pizza from the place near the highway that cuts the slices too big. He loved American pizza and has been bugging me for the same in Russia. Then he wants ice cream even when it's cold. When he has finally had enough junk food, I take him back to my place or Anya's apartment, cartoons blaring while he sprawls on the couch and narrates every episode like I might miss something crucial.

I didn't know life could be this... simple. Or this relaxing. I feel like I'm living in an alternative reality sometimes—a middle-aged dad doing mundane, father-son activities on weekends before rushing off to a dreary office job on Mondays.

Except I don't have a boring job. Or any job, currently.

Dmitry has been running things well. Better than well, if I'm honest. He calls when he needs me. I advise. I step in when it's necessary. Then I step back again.

He was shocked when I left. Shocked again when he found out his girlfriend was pregnant.

She's due soon. A girl, he says. He sounds terrified and proud all at once.

We're all getting together for Christmas. In Moscow at Aleksei's townhouse. I thought Lena would leave me out for certain, but she said I'm invited, along with Anya and Aleksandr. Zorina told her about our visit, and I think both women are convinced I'm going to marry Anya and adopt Aleksandr. It'll be the first time with all of us in the same place. All my brothers, their wives and girlfriends, and children. A house full of noise and life.

For the first time, I don't dread it.

I plan to bring Anya. Aleksandr too.

I plan to tell my family about them. Maybe not the entire truth. But pieces of it.

I'm pulled away from my head by Aleksandr's boots thudding over the ground.

Aleksandr pulls off his helmet and hands it to me like it's a sacred object. "Did you ride horses when you were a kid?"

"No."

"Why not?"

I shrug. "My father didn't want me to."

He frowns, thinking. "I get it. My father never wanted me to do anything but study. But then I found someone like you."

I look his broad grin, like he's proud of himself for walking up to me that day, like he's proud of having me in his life. I tell myself I can't lie to myself. He doesn't know who I really am. His smile is unguarded here, the way he trusts the world when he's on a horse, balanced and brave, is all because he doesn't suspect he's in danger with me.

"You're lucky. Unfortunately," I say with a wry smile. "I never found a kind benefactor like myself."

"What's a benefactor?" Aleksandr asks.

"Someone who helps and supports you. Who makes your dreams come true."

"Like a genie?" His eyes light up.

I scoff. "Sure, like a genie."

"Do you live in a lamp?"

"No, I live in a house. You have seen it."

Aleksandr nods, eyebrows furrowed like he's trying to add all this in his head.

He runs back to the pony to pat its neck, murmuring something only the animal can hear. I watch him, hands in my coat pockets, breathing in the smell of hay and cold air.

I never knew what it felt like to live like this.

And I know, with a clarity that hurts, that when this ends, it will leave a hole in me I won't be able to fill.

WEEKS LATER...

ALEKSEI'S TOWNHOUSE is already loud before we even step inside.

Warmth spills out the moment the door opens. Laughter. Music. The smell of roasted meat, baked bread, citrus, and something sweet burning slightly in the oven. Christmas lights are strung everywhere, along the stair railings and across the wide archways, softening the hard lines of the place.

This house was built to intimidate. Tonight, it feels lived in.

Lena is the first to appear, Anechka balanced on her hip. My sister-in-law pauses when she sees me. The tension is still there, thin as a wire pulled tight, but it does not snap.

Then she sees Anya.

And Aleksandr.

Something in her expression changes.

"Oh," she says softly, eyes warming. She steps forward without hesitation. "You must be Anya."

Anya stiffens beside me, then smiles politely. "Yes."

Lena shifts Anechka to Aleksei, who has come up behind her, and reaches out, squeezing Anya's arm gently. "Welcome. I'm glad you came."

I watch Anya's shoulders loosen just a fraction.

Aleksandr peers up at Lena, then at Anechka, who stares back at him with solemn curiosity.

"Well," Lena adds, crouching slightly, "you must be Aleksandr."

He nods, serious. "Yes."

Aleksei chuckles. "That's our Anechka," he says, lifting his daughter's hand in a small wave. "She's shy, but she likes new friends."

Aleksandr studies her, then gives a tentative wave back.

The knot in my chest eases.

Inside, the townhouse is full.

Mikhail stands near the long dining table, Zorina tucked into his side, her hand resting absently against his chest as she listens to him talk. She looks radiant even in simple knitwear, her dark hair loose, her expression calm and content. Their baby sleeps in a cradle nearby, oblivious to the noise.

Zorina catches sight of Aleksandr and smiles brightly. "There you are," she says, lifting her hand. "I'm happy to see you again."

Aleksandr grins. He remembers her.

Dmitry is perched on the arm of a sofa, one hand protectively braced against his girlfriend's lower back. She is heavily pregnant now, glowing and exhausted, and Dmitry looks equal parts proud and terrified. He notices me and raises a brow.

"Being a pakhan is rough." I slap his back. "I can see that you're barely getting used to it."

"So," Nikolai, my youngest brother, the eternal troublemaker of the family jumps into the conversation, loud enough for everyone to hear, "it's true. You finally stepped down."

I roll my eyes. "Temporarily."

"Temporarily," Dmitry echoes firmly, glancing at the others. "Don't get any ideas. I can't keep doing this forever."

Nikolai laughs from across the room. His girlfriend Clara sits beside him, their child balanced on his knee. Nikolai looks... settled. Less sharp around the edges than he used to be. He only just graduated high school and got his girlfriend pregnant. Now I'm paying for them to attend college in the US. At least one of them seems serious about education, and it's not him. Clara used to be a straight-A student until she fell for the bad boy.

"Didn't think I'd see the day," he calls. "Leo Antonov on holiday."

"I'm not on holiday," I mutter.

"That's what all retired men say," Mikhail adds dryly.

Food is everywhere. Plates passed hand to hand. Someone keeps refilling glasses. Aleksei carves meat while Lena directs traffic with practiced ease. This is not a Bratva gathering. This is a family dinner that happens to include dangerous men.

At some point, the attention shifts.

"So," Nikolai says, nodding toward Anya, "who's this?"

I feel Anya glance at me.

"This is Anya," I say calmly. "An old friend. I'm helping her out for a while. And this is Aleksandr. Her son."

My brothers may be my brothers, but they're all Bratva men. They know bullshit when they hear it. I'm subjected to their suspicious gazes. They know there's more between Anya and me, but for tonight, I'm not answering any questions.

Aleksandr is quickly absorbed into a small group of children. Anechka toddles after him, and Aleksei's son joins them, the three of them sprawled on the rug with toy cars and blocks.

Zorina watches them with a soft smile. "They're good together," she murmurs.

"They are," I agree.

Later, Nikolai leans closer to Anya, curiosity lighting his face. "So what do you do?"

"I used to be a figure skater," Anya replies easily. "Right now, I'm the process of getting a divorce from my husband. Leo is helping me. I'm so grateful for his help."

Nikolai's eyes widen. "Wait." He looks at me. "Didn't Mikhail once say you tried figure skating?"

Anya's lips twitch. "Yes, when we were young. That's how we met."

"No way. That means you know all the embarrassing stories from his youth. How many times did he fall on the ice?"

Anya giggles. "A lot."

"Leo was born to be a Mafioso."

"When we were young," Anya says. "I used to tell him that he could be a champion someday. He was so determined. He came to the rink every day."

Nikolai, always flirty, winks at her. "That's probably because you were there."

Anya blushes. "I wonder."

She's not hiding our relationship with that reaction. I catch Dmitry pursing his lips, calculating in his head how close she is to me. I see Aleksei raise his eyebrows, convinced I'm dating her.

I avoid their gazes and hope the dinner ends soon.

But even I have to admit that Lena's house is warm, and seeing Anya feel at ease with people around her is a sight I'd give anything to see again.

Someone produces a battered Monopoly box from a cupboard like it's a sacred artifact. Lena claps her hands once. "All right. Games. Anyone who doesn't want to lose spectacularly should sit far away from Leo."

"I'm offended," I say dryly.

"You shouldn't be," Lena replies without missing a beat. "You build criminal empires for a living. Nobody would stand a chance."

Anya laughs as she settles at the table with Zorina, Callista, and Clara. They need one more person, so Nikolai drops into a chair beside them, already grinning like he's hosting a private audience.

"I'll play," he says. "I enjoy watching powerful women

bankrupt each other."

"You enjoy flirting," Clara mutters, but there's no heat in it.

Nikolai winks at her. Then at Zorina. Then, daringly, at Anya.

"Careful," Zorina says sweetly. "My husband is very possessive."

Mikhail looks up from his phone. "I am."

Nikolai raises both hands. "Respectfully admiring, then."

They start playing, and the women's cheerful sounds fill the house. Only a few years ago, this house used to be as silent as a tomb. But now the sounds of happy women and children fill the air. I feel like I'm in a different place. This is what I sacrificed my life to build—a huge, happy family that lacks for nothing.

But seeing it in front of my eyes is making my chest tighter.

I slide back on my feet toward the kitchen There are too many people, and I daresay Aleksei and Mikhail will keep Nikolai's excessive flirting in check. Dmitry is already on his laptop, using every spare second to check on our operations.

I pour myself a bourbon and retreat to the kitchen, where the hum of conversation dulls into something manageable. I stare at the walls, the food piled on the counter, and the cake warming in the oven. The small alone makes me want a slice.

Aleksei finds me minutes later. He's huge, though some of his muscle has gone soft since the birth of his children. He looks like a contented man, and once again, I feel a surge of pride. My brothers have found happiness. That is enough for me. I gave them what my father couldn't give me.

He leans against the counter, arms crossed. "So. What's going on?"

I raise an eyebrow. "I'm drinking."

"You know what I mean." His gaze flicks toward the living room. "I'm not buying the 'old friend' story. I've interrogated too many guilty parties. I know when a man is lying. What are you hiding about her?"

I take a slow sip. "Nothing."

"Then why did you never bring her around before? She says you knew each other since you were young."

"Our father didn't approve of her."

"You dated her?"

I clear my throat. "Briefly."

"Why did you never tell anyone?"

"You were all too young. There was no reason to."

"And now she's here. With a kid." Aleksei's eyebrows arch. I know he wants definitive answers, and I should probably be honest with him, but after decades of acting like his boss, not giving him anything more than orders, I find it hard to change our dynamic.

"She's divorcing her husband," I volunteer. "He's a powerful politician, so I'm helping her out. Protecting her so he doesn't try anything."

Aleksei's jaw tightens. "And after that?"

"She wants to live with her parents. In the countryside."

He stares at me. "So you're going to move to the countryside with her and leave everything to Dmitry?"

"I'm not moving to the countryside," I say flatly. "And Dmitry is doing fine."

"He's young. Too young to carry the burdens of the organization. Even you were older than him when you took over."

"He's capable. I'll be watching over him."

I pause, then add, "Petrov agreed to the divorce, and I've pressured him enough to get him agree to give her full custody. In Russia a divorce by mutual consent has no mandatory separation period. After filing, there's a three-month cooling-off window. I'll stay close during that time. Make sure nothing happens."

Aleksei exhales sharply. "Why go this far for a 'friend', even an old one? You gave up your title to babysit her and her son."

"She's the only friend I have," I reply. It's both the truth and a lie. "Being the pakhan for so long, all I have are enemies."

"That's not an answer." Aleksei crosses his arms, giving me that tough look he gives to rival soldiers we capture and torture. "Do you love her or not? Because it's quite clear you two aren't just friends."

I look at him. "I like her. Of course I do. That doesn't mean anything changes."

"It should," he says quietly. "You already told her how you feel, didn't you?"

"Yes."

"And?"

"She doesn't want to marry a gangster. She doesn't want her son growing up in danger. One powerful man already destroyed her. She won't risk another."

Aleksei considers that. "Didn't look like she wanted to stay away tonight."

Before I can respond, Dmitry appears in the doorway, arms folded. He has absolutely been listening.

"You stepped down for her," he says. "You don't do that for nothing. Don't give up now."

I groan in frustration. Finding love has made my brothers nosy. "This is why I should've kept the pakhan title. You all think you get a vote in my personal life now."

"I do," Dmitry pipes up. "I'm the pakhan. I'm your boss."

"No you're not," I assert. "I'm not officially part of the organization anymore. I'm a civilian."

Aleksei grunts. "Like hell you are. You're mixed up with everything. You made Oleg redirect a shipment just yesterday."

"I was helping Dmitry so he doesn't collapse from overwork before Callista gives birth."

"I can't wait to meet our baby, but coming back to you, is that why you don't want to marry Anya? Because there's a child involved?" Dmitry snaps his finger, like he figured it out.

"That's exactly why it's complicated."

"Would you adopt him?" Dmitry asks. "If you married her."

"That would put him in danger."

"It's not like before," Dmitry argues. "Things aren't that chaotic anymore."

Aleksei nods. "And if it comes to it, I'll make sure they're protected. Full detail. Around the clock. It's not ideal, but Lena lives with it. So does Zorina. I daresay Anya will adapt."

I lean back against the counter, staring at the bourbon in my glass. "I hope she changes her mind, but I can't force her."

"You can if you wanted to," Dmitry suggests "You've made people do things they hated more times than I can count. You even pressured our enemies to give up their interests. You're a master manipulator."

"But I don't want to manipulate her," I reply. "If she comes to me, she must come willingly."

Aleksei nods in approval. "At least you have honor."

Dmitry hesitates. "If you married her... would you make the boy your heir? Could you accept him as yours, when you told me you didn't want children?"

The question lands heavier than it should. I glance toward the living room. Nikolai isn't nearby.

"The boy is mine," I say quietly. "Whether I marry her or not."

Aleksei frowns. "What do you mean, yours?"

I close my eyes for a second, then open them. "He's my biological son. I only found out recently."

Silence. My brothers trade glances with each other, taking a beat to process this. Dmitry stares at me like he's recalculating reality. Aleksei runs a hand through his hair.

"Mikhail knows," I add.

"And Nikolai?" Aleksei asks.

"Must never know," I say. "He doesn't know how to keep his mouth shut."

"Alright. I agree with that." Dmitry nods, though he seems to still be in shock. "Are you sure the boy is—"

"I'm certain. I got a paternity test. There's no doubt."

"She hid it well." Aleksei looks at Anya, who is playing monopoly, with an approving smile. "Deceiving Leo Antonov is no easy task. She belongs in the Bratva, after all. She's good at keeping secrets."

"I'm glad you brought her and Aleksandr here tonight," Dmitry says. "It might be our only chance to ever meet them, if your love story doesn't work out."

"Stop being a pessimist." Aleksei hisses at our younger brother.

Aleksei steps closer, resting a hand briefly on my shoulder. "How does it feel to be a father?"

I consider it. "Not terrible.

"Are you planning to bring him into the organization someday? I mean, he's your flesh and blood."

I stiffen. "He won't be in the Bratva. Our father never gave us a choice," I add. "I will. To him. To all of your children, too. I won't force anyone to commit crimes they don't want to."

From the other room, laughter spills over. Anya's laugh, bright and unguarded.

I turn toward the sound without meaning to.

For the first time in a long while, the future doesn't feel like a battlefield. The laughter isn't forced. It flows freely, filling the space, like it was always meant to. Happiness swells, only broken by the crying of small children.

It feels like the family I've always dreamed of.

TWENTY-TWO

Anya

ELEVEN YEARS AGO...

I FOUND THEM BY ACCIDENT.

That is the lie I tell myself later, because the truth feels worse. The truth is that something in me already knew. Knew the moment Igor looked at the silver-haired woman, when she gave him her number under the guise of a business deal, that it would lead to more. I was too shaken by Leo's proposal to care.

But last week, I discovered messages between them on his phone. And I know they're meeting here tonight. I hope against my better sense that it's just a business meeting, that they're just signing a deal.

The hotel corridor is hushed, carpet swallowing my steps as I follow the sound of low laughter, the familiar cadence of his voice. I tell myself I am only looking for Igor. That I want to ask him about the seating chart. About the photographer. About anything that makes me feel like a bride instead of a guest in my own life.

Our wedding is days away, and I don't want to discover that my fiancé has been cheating on me. I don't even have to use the copy of the room's key card that I got made through an illegal source.

The door is already ajar. I push it open, stepping in.

The woman in the silver dress is pressed against the wall, her hair loose now, her lipstick smeared. Igor Petrov's hands are on her waist, his mouth at her neck. He murmurs something that makes her laugh softly, breathlessly.

My heart drops so hard I feel it in my knees.

"Igor," I say. It should have been a scream. My heart should be burning, raging with anger. My throat tightens, but not with tears or rage. With panic.

But I realize I'm thinking more about how much cancelling the wedding will cost. I don't love Igor Petrov. I never have and never will. That's why I feel nothing except betrayal and worry about my future.

He freezes when he notices I'm in the room. The woman turns, eyes widening. For a second, all three of us stare at one another in the mirror by the door. I take in everything with cruel clarity. The undone buttons on his shirt. The flush on his throat. The way he does not look ashamed, only startled.

"Oh," the woman says quickly. "I should go."

She brushes past me, avoiding my eyes. Her perfume lingers, sharp and sweet. The door clicks shut behind her, and the room feels smaller, suffocating.

Igor runs a hand through his hair. "Anya, listen."

"How long?" My voice sounds calm. That frightens me more than if I were screaming.

"It was nothing," he says immediately. "A momentary lapse of judgment. I had too much to drink. It meant nothing."

"You kissed her," I say. "Days before our wedding."

He steps closer, hands raised as if I am a skittish animal. "I made a mistake. That is all. It will not happen again. I promise you. If you had watched for longer, you'd have seen that I'd never have gone all the way. I would have come to my senses before that. I could never betray you."

He's evading me. He still hasn't answered my question about how long this affair has been going on. And I don't want to push. I want to believe his sweet lies, trust that he kissed her for the first time today and he'd have come to his senses before things got out of hand.

I should walk out. I should end it. But the calendar flashes in my mind. The invitations sent. The guests flying in. My parents' pride. The quiet understanding that I have already quit my career, already reshaped my life around this decision.

I rejected Leo, too. He offered me a way out of this, and now I don't even have that to fall back on. Not that I would pick him. I still haven't forgiven him for treating me so callously that day, even if he apologized. At least his apology had sincerity, which is not something Igor will ever give me.

"You cannot do this again," I say. My chest aches. "I cannot back out now."

"I won't," he says quickly. "I swear it. You will be my wife. I will be faithful."

I nod, because I do not know what else to do.

THE WEDDING DAY arrives like a performance I have rehearsed too many times to escape.

My dress is ivory silk, fitted at the bodice, flowing like water when I walk. My mother cries as she buttons me in, telling me how lucky I am. My aunt kisses my cheek and says I have found such a rich, handsome, amazing man. They smile with relief, with pride. They do not see the tightness in my chest, the way my hands tremble when I hold the bouquet.

As I walk down the aisle, I think of another room, another night. Leo standing in the shadows, eyes dark, voice low as he told me he wanted to marry me. I remember the way my pride flared, the way I turned away because I would not be the woman who came back only when it was convenient. The way his eyes were filled with deep regret when he apologized for the past, not the nothingness Igor's eyes were filled with when he said he'd never cheat on me again. I would trust Leo with my soul. But my husband? I can't say the same for him.

Should I have swallowed my pride? Should I have gone to Leo and married him after I found out Igor cheated?

I tell myself no. I tell myself this was not a mistake. Igor promised me and he might change for the better. People deserve second chances. Besides, I don't want to get shot again. Leo is playing with very dangerous people now. I don't want to be involved in crime. I just want an easy, comfortable, safe life.

Igor looks perfectly polished at the altar. He's smiling—that politician smile. I begin to wonder if any of his smiles were every genuine, or if he was always playing a character. Was I too stupid to see through his mask?

I ask myself that question again and again as I say my vows. Igor Petrov says his. The applause washes over us like noise through glass.

There are so many guests. I am tired by the time we've danced, had dinner, and celebrated with all of them. It's painful smiling when I feel so unsure on the inside. Everybody thinks I got a prize by marrying a promising politician. If it had been Leo instead, I doubt my parents would have come. They'd have criticized me for picking a gangster. But maybe I'd have been happier even without anybody's approval or blessing. All I can do now is wonder about the choice I was too prideful to make.

After the wedding the reception, I excuse myself to get some air.

It's late at night. All the guests have gone home except my parents. I send them home, assuring them my husband and I will be fine. All I need to do is find my husband and spend the night in his arms. Our wedding night might be the last chance of restoring our relationship, though the mere thought of having sex with him after what I saw makes my stomach turn.

But Igor is nowhere to be found. I scan the venue, running desperately in high heels.

Then I see it. It's the same woman I saw at the hotel. She was a wedding guest, but I was gracious because I believed she would stop if she saw Igor put a ring on me.

But neither my husband nor she had any intention of changing.

My lungs burn as I see them again before I even register what I am looking at. Igor has her cornered near the terrace, his hand cupping her jaw. He kisses her openly, lazily, as if daring the world to object.

Our eyes meet. He knows I'm looking.

But he does not stop.

Something inside me breaks cleanly, like a bone snapping under pressure.

Tears exert pressure behind my eyeballs. I can't stand this anymore. I can't run to my parents' house, either, or my aunt's. They think I married a gentleman. I can't disappoint them so soon.

There's only one person I know who'll let me stay at their place. Leo Antonov.

I run.

I do not remember the drive. Only the blur of lights, the weight of the dress, the way my breath comes apart in my chest. I stop in front of Leo's townhouse, my veil crooked, my hands shaking as I ring the bell.

He opens the door and stares at me like I am a ghost. "Anya? Did you get married today?"

I nod, but he sees the tears streaking down my face. And he doesn't ask for details, just lets me into his house.

"Did he hurt you?" He brings me a glass of water, and wipes my tears.

"No. He cheated on me. On our wedding day. Can you believe that? Even when I caught him, he didn't stop." I gulp down the water, but my throat continues to sting. It's sore from crying.

Leo puts his arms around me, enveloping me in masculine safety. I think I forgot what that felt like after two years with Petrov. I never felt safe in his arms. He held me like a fragile doll, like he couldn't wait to let go of me.

Leo holds me like he never wants to stop hugging me.

"You can divorce him," Leo says.

"No," I reply. "I can't. He said he would change."

"Do you really believe that?"

I laugh, a bitter sound. "I guess I'll have to become like all political wives, then—turning a blind eye to his affairs."

"Anya..." Leo's words disappear with a loud exhale. He strokes my back as I cling to his warm arms, crying like a child. At any appoint, he could have told me that he was right. He said a cold, practical marriage would kill me, and he knew me all along.

But Leo isn't egotistical or arrogant. He cares for me. How stupid I was to ignore his feelings. To ignore mine.

"Leo." I reach behind and unzip my gown. "I want to feel

you inside me tonight. I want you to be the man who fucks me on my wedding night. My husband doesn't deserve that honor anymore."

"Anya," he says hoarsely. "You are married."

"I know," I whisper. Tears spill down my face. "Please. Just... make me feel better. One last time."

His jaw tightens. "I cannot."

His eyes are haunted. Uncertain. I realize I can sway him. I can make him give me what I need. I cradle his face, pushing my face up until our lips meet.

It is desperate and clumsy, my mouth trembling against his. For a heartbeat, he does nothing. Then his hands come up, gripping my waist, pulling me closer. He kisses me back with a hunger that feels like punishment and mercy all at once.

"I love you," I breathe against his mouth. "I was too stupid to see it until it was too late."

He rests his forehead against mine, eyes closed, breathing hard. "You should leave."

"I do not care," I say. "I cannot go back to him tonight. Tomorrow, I'll go back forever and resign myself to my fate. I'm not so cruel that I'd keep stringing you along, making you do something that goes against your morals. But let me have you today. I want to know what I could have had."

Silence stretches between us, thick and heavy with everything we have lost. Then he slides the sleeves of my gown off my shoulders, exposing my bare breasts.

"You look so lovely." He takes my hand, kissing the ring on it. "How I wish I could have put this ring on you."

Tears well in my eyes again.

Leo's mouth closes over my nipple, hot and wet, sucking hard enough to make me gasp. His teeth graze the sensitive peak, sending sparks of pleasure straight between my legs. I arch into him, my hands fisting in his hair.

"Leo," I breathe.

He switches to my other breast, lavishing it with the same attention. His hand slides down my stomach, over my hip, finding the heat between my thighs. His fingers brush against my wetness, and I hear him groan.

"Open your legs," he commands, his voice rough. "Let me see your pussy."

I obey, trembling as I spread my thighs for him. His eyes darken as he looks at me, at how wet and swollen I am.

"Perfect," he mutters. "So fucking perfect."

Before I can respond, he stands and throws me over his shoulder like I weigh nothing. I yelp in surprise, my hands scrambling against his back.

"Leo!"

His palm comes down hard on my bare ass, the crack of it echoing in the room. The sting blooms into heat, and I gasp.

"You came to me for rough sex," he says, his voice hard. "Not for the gentle kind your husband gives you."

I laugh breathlessly. "I guess it's better being carried over your shoulder than being carried bride-style by him."

He brings me to his bedroom and tosses me onto the bed. I bounce once, my hair spilling around me, my body on display for him. He stands at the foot of the bed, his eyes roaming over every inch of me.

Then he kneels. He looks dominant even when he's below me. That's how powerful Leo Antonov is. He's a storm, a force of nature, and he's going to make sure my pussy feels every ounce of his wrath tonight. I took another man's name, another man's ring. But even so, at the core of me, I will remain his forever. Our love will bind us together.

His hands wrap around my ankle, lifting my leg. He presses a kiss to the arch of my foot, then another to my ankle. His lips trail up my calf, soft and deliberate, until he reaches the sensitive skin of my inner thigh.

"Beautiful," he murmurs against my skin.

His mouth moves higher, kissing, sucking, biting gently. When he reaches the apex of my thighs, he pauses, his breath hot against my wetness.

"Please," I whisper.

His tongue flicks out, drawing a slow circle around my clit. I cry out, my hips jerking off the bed. He holds me down with one strong hand, his tongue working me with maddening precision.

He licks and sucks, alternating between soft strokes and firm pressure. My hands fly to his hair, gripping tight as pleasure builds inside me like a storm.

"Leo, I'm going to—"

He doesn't stop. He intensifies his efforts, his tongue circling my clit faster, his fingers sliding inside me, curling to hit that spot that makes my vision blur.

I shatter.

The orgasm crashes over me in waves, my body convulsing, my mind going blank. I see stars, feel myself floating, the world forgotten. There's nothing but this—the pleasure, the release, the way he makes me feel alive.

When I come back to myself, I'm boneless, my breathing ragged. Leo is watching me, his lips glistening with my arousal.

"My husband," I say weakly, "has never made me come. Not once. You've spoiled me for all men."

A satisfied smile curves his lips. "Good."

He stands, his hands going to his belt. "Do you remember what I told you when we got back together?"

I blink up at him, dazed. "What?"

"I said I'd make sure you're carrying my baby, even if we don't end up together."

My breath catches as he pushes his pants down, revealing his cock. It's thick and hard, the tip glistening with precum. I stare, my mouth going dry.

"Take a good look," he says, his voice dark and possessive. "This is the cock that's going to impregnate you on your wedding night."

Heat floods through me at his words. It's wrong. I know it's wrong. But the idea of carrying Petrov's child is abhorrent. This—this feels right.

"I want it," I whisper. "I want to be bred by you. I want you to fill me with your seed until I'm leaking."

His eyes flash. "You're my breeding slut, aren't you? Can't wait for me to stuff you full of cum."

He climbs onto the bed, pushing my legs apart. He positions himself at my entrance, the thick head of his cock pressing against my wetness.

"You're going to take every inch," he growls. "You're going to carry my child, and when Petrov looks at you, he'll never know."

He thrusts inside in one hard stroke, filling me completely. I scream, my nails digging into his shoulders. He's so big, stretching me, claiming me.

"That's it," he groans. "Stretch for my cock like a good girl. You know how big I am, but you always take me so well."

He pins my wrists above my head with one hand, his other gripping my hip hard enough to bruise. He pulls out and slams back in, setting a brutal pace that has the headboard banging against the wall.

"You're mine," he says through gritted teeth. "This pussy is mine. This body is mine. No matter whose ring you're wearing, your womb will only carry my child."

"Yes," I gasp. "Oh my God. Your cock is hitting all the right spots."

He pounds into me, each thrust hitting deeper than the last.

I can feel him everywhere, can feel the way my body yields to him, takes him, welcomes him.

"I'm going to fill you," he growls. "Going to pump you so full of my cum you'll be dripping for days."

The dirty talk sends me spiraling toward another orgasm. I clench around him, my body tightening.

"Come on my cock," he demands. "Come while I breed you."

I do. My second orgasm is even more intense than the first, ripping through me with such force that I can't even scream. My body locks up, my pussy milking his cock.

He follows me over the edge with a roar, burying himself as deep as possible. I feel the hot pulse of his release filling me, marking me, claiming me in the most primal way.

He collapses on top of me, both of us breathing hard. After a moment, he rolls to the side, pulling me with him. His hand rests on my stomach, possessive and tender.

"If you get pregnant," he says quietly, "I want you to tell me."

I nod, unable to speak past the lump in my throat.

Tomorrow, I'll go back to my husband. Tomorrow, I'll resume my role as Mrs. Petrova.

But tonight, I'm Leo's. And if there's a child growing inside me because of this night, it will be his—always his, even if no one else ever knows.

TWENTY-THREE

Leo

THE DIVORCE PAPERS sit on Petrov's desk like a confession.

I watch him sign them, his hand steady despite the tremor I know is hiding beneath his politician's composure. The office smells like leather and desperation. Outside the window, Moscow spreads gray and indifferent, the city that has witnessed a thousand betrayals and will witness a thousand more.

"There," he says, sliding the papers across to me. "It's done."

I don't touch them yet. I lean back in the chair, studying him. He's aged poorly. The lines around his mouth are deeper, his eyes duller. Whatever power he once wielded has been stripped away piece by piece over the past months.

My doing.

"Full custody to Anya," I confirm. "No visitation rights. No contact."

"Yes," he says tightly.

"And the financial settlement?"

"Everything she asked for." His jaw works. "You've made sure I have no choice."

I smile. It's not a kind smile. "That was the point."

He looks at me with something like hatred, but mostly defeat. "You destroyed me."

"You destroyed yourself," I correct. "You abused your wife. You beat your son. I just made sure the consequences found you."

He swallows. "Is she... with you now?"

"That's none of your concern."

His hands clench into fists on the desk. "Aleksandr isn't even mine, is he? When I looked at you next to him at the party, I realized he looked a lot like you."

"Is that why you beat him after? And her, too? Because you were scared he was mine and she had lied to you?"

Petrov clears his throat. "The bitch never came clean, though. But now I'm almost sure. You wouldn't go so far otherwise."

The question hangs in the air. I could lie. I could let him keep that small dignity. But I need him to give up on Aleksandr forever, to not ask for visitation rights later down the line. If he knows Aleksandr is not his son, he won't be interested in being a part of the boy's life anymore.

Instead, I lean forward. "Aleksandr is not you son. He's mine. Biologically. On your wedding night, after you cheated on Anya, she came to me."

The color drains from his face. "How long have you known?"

"Does it matter?"

"She made a fool of me," he says, voice rising. "All these years, I raised another man's—"

"You raised no one," I interrupt coldly. "You terrorized them. Don't pretend you were a father."

He opens his mouth, then closes it. There's nothing left to say.

I stand, gathering the papers. "If you ever try to contact Anya or Aleksandr again, I will finish what I started. Do you understand?"

He nods once, defeated.

I leave his office without looking back.

Outside, my car is waiting. I slide into the back seat, and my driver pulls away from the curb. I pull out my phone and call Anya. Then I hang up. I need her to sign the papers, and she must submit them.

Only then will she be truly free.

SHE COMES out of the courthouse with Aleksandr's hand clenched in hers, knuckles white, shoulders shaking like she's holding herself together with thread.

The building behind her is squat and bureaucratic, all concrete and dull glass. A районный суд, one of a hundred like it in Moscow. No grandeur. No drama. Just stamped papers and bored clerks who decide the fate of lives between lunch breaks.

She looks smaller standing on the steps, coat hanging loose on her frame, eyes red and shining. Aleksandr glances up at her, confused, then back at me, as if checking whether this is a good thing or a bad one.

I step forward before she can see me clearly.

"They accepted everything," she says, voice breaking before she can finish the sentence. "The official said... since Petrov agreed, it's filed through ZAGS. There's a three-month cooling-off period. After that, the divorce is finalized automatically unless someone contests it."

She laughs weakly, disbelieving. "Three months. And then... that's it."

Her knees buckle.

I catch her before she can fall.

She presses her face into my chest, sobbing like the sound has been trapped inside her for years and finally found a crack to escape through.

"I don't have to go back," she whispers. "Leo, I don't have to go back there. He can't touch me anymore. He can't touch Aleksandr."

Aleksandr wraps his arms around her waist, small hands clutching her coat. "Mama?"

She sinks to her knees and pulls him into her arms, kissing his hair again and again. "It's okay. It's okay now."

I crouch beside them, one hand steady on her back, rubbing slow circles, grounding her. Her tears soak through my shirt. I don't move.

"You're free," I say quietly. "You should thank him."

She pulls back just enough to look at me, eyes swollen, incredulous. "Thank him?"

"Aleksandr," I say. "He's the one who asked me to help you."

Her breath stutters. She turns to her son, cupping his face with trembling hands. "You were so brave," she whispers. "So much braver than me."

Then she turns back to me and throws her arms around my neck.

"No," she says fiercely. "I should thank you. You did this. Without you, I would still be his prisoner. I never believed he would let us go."

"I promised you," I say into her hair. "And I don't break promises."

She pulls back, searching my face. "You really think he'll stay away?"

"He knows about Aleksandr. He isn't interested anymore. You know he's traditional," I say coldly. "He won't come near either of you again."

Anya sniffles. "Did you tell him?"

"Yes. I needed him to let Aleksandr go. And it worked."

The word settles between us, heavy and undeniable.

Her lips part. Fresh tears spill over. She presses her forehead to my chest again, fingers gripping my coat like I might disappear if she lets go.

"I never thought you'd protect me after all these years," she whispers. "I chose another man over you, but you always loved me. I don't deserve your love, Leo. You're a man whose heart is bigger than mine. Bigger than anyone I know."

"You don't give yourself enough credit," I reply. "You're very lovable."

I hold her shoulders, steadying her. "You don't have to be afraid anymore."

She laughs weakly through tears. "I don't even know how to live without fear."

"You'll learn," I say. "With time."

She looks up at me then, really looks, and I see the question forming before she speaks it.

"So now what?" she asks softly.

"Now," I say, "you're no man's wife."

Her breath catches.

"And that means," I continue, "I can pursue you freely."

She gives a watery, disbelieving smile. "Why would you pursue a divorcee with a child?"

"Because I love you," I say simply. "Because I still believe the best outcome is you living with me. As a family."

Her expression tightens. "Leo—"

"You saw my family," I interrupt gently. "At Christmas. The women. The children. They're not in danger."

"They're Bratva wives," she says quietly. "They grew up knowing what this life is."

"Lena and Callista were regular American woman who didn't even know what Bratva meant," I counter. "Even so, they haven't had any problems. I still regret that I let you get shot in the past, and maybe that's why, I considered letting you go. But my brother reminded me that I'm a different man now. Back then, I was alone. I had no power, no subordinates, no bodyguards. That's not the case anymore. I have my brothers. I have money. I have influence. Things are different now."

She looks away, blinking hard. "I don't know if I belong in your family."

"Come on. Zorina and Lena love you." I take her hands in mine. "I once told you that if I love you, my family will love you too. That hasn't changed. Aleksei will put men on you and Aleksandr. They will make sure no harm comes to either of you. It will be a bit of an adjustment, but you're used to being a political wife, used to being watched. It won't be much different."

She swallows. "What if I regret it? What if it doesn't work out? I can't divorce you like I divorced Petrov. I don't have that kind of power."

"You won't be trapped," I say firmly. "I won't cage you the way he did. But don't walk a lonely path with Aleksandr when you don't have to. Be with people who will protect you. Who will love you. You have endured abuse and neglect for so long. Give yourself a chance to live a happy life, instead of a safe, mediocre one."

Her shoulders shake again. She nods once, unable to speak.

I pull her into my chest and hold her while she cries, my hand firm and steady at her back, murmuring reassurances I've never said aloud before.

"You don't have to decide immediately," I tell her. "I plan to court you properly for three months. You can give me your answer when your divorce is finalized."

She holds on, her fingers tightening around my bicep. "Leo, I don't deserve your love. Your heart is so big, so generous. How can I ever be worthy of you?"

"You are already worthy of me." I kiss her forehead. "You have protected my son on your own for a decade. And you are the woman I can't stop loving."

TWENTY-FOUR

Anya

PRESENT

LEO'S HAND closes around mine as he guides me toward the jet, firm and warm, like he's afraid I'll change my mind if he lets go.

My heels click softly against the carpeted floor of the private terminal, the sound swallowed by thick walls and muted light. Everything here is hushed, discreet, expensive in a way that doesn't need to announce itself. The kind of place where people like Leo move without being seen.

I glance at him from the corner of my eye. He's dressed simply, dark coat, tailored trousers, no tie. He looks calm. Confident. Like this is nothing.

Like he hasn't spent the last three weeks trying very hard to win me.

And maybe that's the problem.

Three months. I gave him three months like it was a trial period, like I was some impartial judge weighing evidence. At the time, it felt reasonable. Safe. Now, walking beside him, I feel a stab of guilt twist low in my stomach.

Because I owe my freedom to him. I owe my life and my son's life to him. And he's been trying to prove he deserves more than gratitude. When she shouldn't have to prove anything at all. Deep in my heart, I'm certain I love him. I want him more than I've wanted anyone. Even one failed and abusive marriage isn't enough to put me off the idea of being with Leo. But not as his wife. That's a huge commitment, and I'm not sure I can make that. But I want to be his partner, be the woman he comes home to at the end of a hard day. I want to soothe his worries and take care of him. I want to have sex with him and wake up in his arms the next morning, knowing I'm exactly where I belong.

The first date flashes through my mind as we reach the stairs of the jet.

He took me to Paris.

He didn't tell me where we were going. Just told me to pack something warm and something beautiful. We walked along the Seine at night, the city glowing gold and alive, his coat draped over my shoulders when the wind picked up. Dinner in a quiet restaurant where the chef came out to greet him by name, and Leo pretended not to notice my disbelief.

"You don't have to do this," I'd told him over wine, my fingers tracing the rim of the glass.

"I know," he'd replied. "I want to."

That was the thing. He always wanted to. Unlike my ex-husband, who only did the bare minimum, who always gave love with a goal in mind, Leo gave his affections freely with no agenda. After decades, she still helped me even though he had nothing to gain from it.

The second date had been quieter. Florence. A villa tucked into the hills, olive trees and warm stone, no guards in sight even though I knew they were there. He cooked for me. Leo Antonov, ruler of empires, standing barefoot in a kitchen, chopping garlic and asking if I preferred rosemary or thyme.

"You're spoiling me," I'd said, laughing as he plated the food like it mattered.

"That's right," he'd answered, not smiling. "Are you starting to see the benefits of being my lover now?"

The third date had been yesterday.

Moscow, but not the Moscow that hurt. Not the Moscow that terrified me when I was young. It's as though he wanted to show me that even though the city was his same, he wasn't the same man anymore. He has power now, and bodyguards who keep an eye out for any enemy attacks. They trailed us quietly as we made our way to a private gallery opening, closed to the public.

In a way, I realized I had been holding onto the past for too long. We had both been young then. He was dating me against his father's wishes. He had nobody working under him, and he was an easy target as the pakhan's son. I was just an up-and-coming figure skater, with no big medals to my name. I already felt like I didn't have enough in the world. I loved Leo when he was young, but we have both clearly come a long way since then.

"I have peace treaties in place with most of the other gangs now," Leo told me, putting a hand on my shoulder, as if trying to announce to everybody there that I was his. I laughed. I'm just a middle-aged woman, way past her prime. There's nothing special about me, but he treats me like I'm a woman whom everybody desires, and he's the only one lucky enough to be chosen by. "They won't attack me, or they risk getting torn apart in return. The Antonov Bratva's name is feared these days. I still have enemies, malishka, but I'm not somebody they can touch easily."

We wandered between paintings while a pianist played softly in the corner. Leo had stopped in front of a canvas, something abstract and violent and beautiful all at once. I didn't think he was the type who enjoyed art, but he is more sensitive than I gave him credit for. Maybe I'm the one who needs to change my biases.

"This is how my life feels when I'm not with you," he'd said quietly. "Chaos pretending to be control."

I'd looked at him then, really looked, and remembered every reason I had ever loved him.

Strong. Damaged. Loyal to the bone. Dangerous, but never to me. The only man I respected. The only man I'd bow to willingly, because I trusted him not to use my submission as a weapon against me.

Leo Antonov is domineering, controlling, and according to his brothers' wives, patriarchal. But he's not cruel or demeaning, nor will he take away the voice of anyone he truly loves. He has never treated a woman badly in his life, and if that doesn't speak volumes about a man's character, I don't know what does. To me, he is masculine perfection.

I step onto the jet, the soft hum of readiness vibrating beneath my feet. Aleksandr darts ahead of us, practically bouncing.

"Where are we going?" he asks for the third time in two minutes. "America again? Or somewhere cooler? Do they have guns there?"

"Absolutely not," I say automatically, even as Leo lets out a low huff of amusement.

Aleksandr grins up at him. "You didn't say no."

Leo arches a brow. "I also didn't say yes."

That only seems to encourage him.

Watching them together still does something strange to my chest. Aleksandr watches Leo like he's made of legend. Like everything Leo says matters. Like he's already decided that this is what a man should be.

And I wonder, not for the first time, if I'm stealing something from my son.

I don't want him to grow up in violence. I don't want guns to be toys or power to be measured in fear. I want him safe. Ordinary. Free.

But Leo lives in a world that is none of those things.

And yet, when I look at Leo with Aleksandr, patient and dry and unexpectedly gentle, I don't see a monster. I see a man who never had a choice, trying desperately to give one to the people he loves.

Including my son. Sometimes, I wonder if I'm being overprotective by stealing Aleksandr's chance at having a father figure who actually wants him to thrive. I am a dedicated mother, and I will do everything for my son, but maybe the burden of doing everything has made me overl paranoid.

That scares me more than the alternative.

I squeeze Leo's hand without thinking. He looks down at me, questioning.

"You okay?" he asks softly.

"I think I was unfair to you," I admit. "Three months is very short."

His mouth curves, just barely. "I've accomplished more in less time."

"I can't decide if your overconfidence is endearing or annoying." I swallow. "And I keep wondering if I'm doing the right thing for Aleksandr."

Leo's expression shifts, something serious settling into

place. "I won't turn him into me."

"I know," I say quickly. "I just... he looks at you like you hung the sun. And he's fascinated by your world. By guns. By power."

Leo exhales slowly. "He's a boy. He's curious. That doesn't mean he has to become what I am."

I want to believe that.

I do believe that.

We move deeper into the cabin. Plush seats, soft light, a quiet luxury that feels unreal even now. Freedom still feels unreal sometimes. Divorce papers signed. No one waiting for me with anger in their eyes. No fear of footsteps behind me.

And yet, in the quiet moments, I miss having someone to share it with. Someone to sit beside me when Aleksandr sleeps. Someone to carry the weight with me.

Leo watches me like he already knows all of this.

Aleksandr flops into a seat, kicking his feet. "So. Where are we actually going?"

Leo finally answers, voice calm. "Somewhere with horses."

Aleksandr beams. "That sounds awesome."

I close my eyes for a moment as the door seals shut.

I don't know if I'm right.

I don't know if love is enough to bridge the gap between the life Leo lives and the life I want for my son.

But as the engines begin to hum and Leo's hand tightens around mine, I know one thing with aching clarity.

I don't think Leo Antonov is a bad man.

And I don't think loving him is a mistake.

TWENTY-FIVE

Leo

"I CAN'T BELIEVE you let him ride horses."

Anya says it like an accusation, but there's no real heat in it. Just disbelief and something softer underneath.

I watch Aleksandr circle the paddock on a chestnut pony, helmet slightly too big, posture stiff with concentration. The riding school stretches out around us in rolling green acres, hedges trimmed within an inch of their lives, fences white and immaculate. Beyond the fields rises an old English manor, all stone and ivy and quiet authority. The kind of place where history breathes through the walls.

"It's a good hobby. Rich people do it all the time." I say calmly.

She shoots me a look. "That's your justification?"

"It'll be good for his future," I reply. "He can make friends with other upper class kids instead of thugs like me. Isn't that what you want for him?"

Anya frowns, and hisses. "There will be no upper class kids in my parents' hometown."

"But what about later? What if he wants to go to high school abroad? When he goes to college? I'll pay for his education, Anya. I don't want you to worry about money. He's still my son, and he should get the best."

Anya opens her mouth to protest. I'm sure she was planning to say she doesn't need my money, but my son interrupts at the perfect time.

Aleksandr spots us and lifts one hand, wobbling a little as he does. "Mama! Mr. Leo!"

She waves back instantly, smile breaking free despite herself. Pride shines in her eyes, naked and unguarded. She tries to hide it by crossing her arms.

"He looks happy," she murmurs.

"He is," I say. Then I divert her attention, pointing to the English castle in the distance. "We're staying there tonight, by the way. As guests. It used to be an earl's estate in the past but now it's a hotel, and it's part of this riding school. Guests can get riding lessons for free. That includes us."

Her head snaps toward me. There's dry humor in her expression, like she's trying hard to hate me, and she's failing miserably. "I'm not even surprised at the extravagant things you plan anymore."

"The instructors here are world-class," I add. "Former Olympians. Aleksandr can ride as long as he wants."

She exhales slowly. "How long has this been going on? You said you took him to riding lessons in Moscow."

"It started after he asked me about horses in Las Vegas," I admit. "Right after the amusement park. You made me babysit him every Saturday, and that was the perfect cover."

"I always thought you'd be strict and tough as a dad." Her lips press together. "But you're an overly indulgent father.

Any time he asks anything, you just jump up like a dog and let him have it. He needs to learn that he can't have everything in life."

I arch a brow. "Malishka, he's *my* son. He can have everything in life."

She scoffs. "You're incorrigible. I hope Aleksandr doesn't grow up to be a spoiled kid."

"I'm sure you'll keep him on track. He's pretty sensitive, thanks to your parenting. I guess spending a lot of time around you made him keenly aware of emotions."

"No, he gets that from you," Anya retorts. "You always know what everyone is thinking and feeling just by looking at them. I could never lie to you, because you always picked up whenever I was sad."

Aleksandr completes another loop and beams when the instructor praises him. He looks older somehow. Taller. Less closed in on himself.

"He used to barely speak to Petrov," Anya says quietly. "He was withdrawn. Careful. I thought that was just his personality."

"He ran to my car the first time he saw me in that parking lot," I say. "Like he'd been waiting."

Her eyes glisten.

"He's bloomed," she whispers. "Since you came back into our lives."

I glance at her, then away. "Fathers and sons are allowed to have secrets."

Her breath catches.

I immediately regret the words.

"That came out wrong," I say, turning to her. "I'm sorry. I wasn't trying to undermine you. You're the one who raised him. You did everything. I know that."

She steps closer and wraps her arms around me, face

pressed into my chest. "I don't feel undermined," she says softly. "I feel... relieved. Grateful. He finally trusts someone."

I rest my chin lightly against her hair. "Will you ever tell him?"

She pulls back just enough to look at me. "That depends."

"On what?"

"On whether you can woo me successfully or not."

I snort. "So my fate is sealed."

The instructor approaches, smiling. "I'm taking Aleksandr on a tour of the grounds. If you'd like, you can follow on horseback as well."

"I trust he's in good hands," I say.

Aleksandr looks thrilled. "Really?"

"Yes," I tell him. "Go."

He rides off, chattering excitedly.

I slide my hand around Anya's waist, drawing her close. "It's time we let our son have some independence."

Her eyes flick up to mine. "Our son?"

"Habit," I say smoothly. "Come on. Let's see our room."

She laughs under her breath as I steer her toward the manor, the afternoon sun warming stone and grass alike.

THE ROOM IS ABSURD.

That's the first thought that crosses my mind as I push open the heavy oak door. Vaulted ceilings stretch overhead, painted with faded murals of pastoral scenes—shepherds and sheep, clouds and cherubs. A four-poster bed dominates the center, draped in burgundy silk that catches the afternoon light filtering through tall windows. The floor is polished wood, partially covered by Persian rugs so old they've worn soft at the edges. A fireplace sits against the far wall, stone mantle carved with the estate's crest, flames already crackling low and warm.

"This is ridiculous," Anya says, stepping inside. Her voice echoes slightly.

"It's worthy of a queen like you," I correct.

She coughs like I made a joke. "I'm not a queen."

"I'm the king of an underworld empire and you're dating me." I take her hand and press a kiss, holding her gaze. "You're my queen. That's close enough."

I close the door behind us, the lock clicking with a satisfying finality. "Besides, I want to show you the life I can give you."

"I don't need the material luxuries. They don't matter to me anymore. I've had enough of those for a lifetime."

"I know. Those are not the only things I'm offering you. My love and devotion will always be yours, Anya, until the day we die. I've never been with any other woman. Even when you were married, and I didn't think I could have you, I didn't want to be with anyone else."

I see the way Anya's lips tremble, the slight narrowing of her eyes. "I'm sorry I put you through that."

"You told me once that some people are only destined to find true love once in their lifetime. That we found ours with each other. Do you still believe it?"

Anya swallows. I watch the smooth column of her throat bulge. "I don't know if I have the right to believe that anymore."

She turns to face me, one eyebrow raised, arms crossed. But there's a softness in her eyes that wasn't there before. Trust. Contentment. Maybe even happiness. And also fear.

I cross to her slowly, deliberately, giving her time to move away if she wants. She doesn't.

My hands find her waist, fingers sliding beneath the hem of her sweater. "Let me see you," I murmur.

Her breath hitches. "Leo—"

I kiss her before she can finish the protest.

It's slow this time. Deliberate. My mouth moves over hers with the patience I've learned over years of waiting for her. I taste her bottom lip, suck it gently, feel her melt against me. Her hands come up to grip my shoulders, steadying herself.

When I pull back, her lips are swollen, eyes dark.

I lift her sweater over her head, revealing smooth skin and the simple white bra beneath. My fingers trace the line of her collarbone, down to the swell of her breasts.

"Beautiful," I say quietly.

I unhook her bra, letting it fall. Her breasts spill free, full and soft, nipples already tight. I lower my head, pressing a kiss to the curve of her shoulder, then another to her collarbone. My lips trail down to her chest, pausing at the top of one breast before I take her nipple into my mouth.

She gasps, arching into me.

I suck gently, then harder, listening to the sounds she makes —soft moans, sharp inhales, my name whispered like a prayer.

My hands move to her jeans, unbuttoning them, sliding them down over her hips. She steps out of them, leaving her in just her panties.

I kneel in front of her.

Her eyes widen. "Leo, what—"

"I need to ask you something," I say, looking up at her.

She swallows. "Now?"

"Yes." I press a kiss to her stomach, just above the waistband of her panties. "Did you make Petrov stop hounding me at the St. Petersburg port all those years ago?"

Her breath catches. She hesitates, then nods slowly. "Yes."

"Why?" I ask. "You were dating him. We had just broken up. You had no reason to help me."

She looks away, cheeks flushing. "I was angry with you. But I still cared. I couldn't stand seeing you suffer."

My chest tightens. "You're the kindest person I've ever met."

"Leo—"

I hook my fingers into her panties and pull them down. She steps out of them, completely bare before me now.

"From the day we first met," I say, pressing a kiss to her inner thigh, "you've always tried to help me."

I spread her legs gently, positioning myself between them. My mouth finds her pussy, already wet and ready. I lick slowly, tasting her, savoring the way she trembles.

"Leo," she gasps, her hands flying to my hair.

I circle her clit with my tongue, teasing it, building her up. Her hips rock against my mouth, seeking more. I give it to her, sucking her clit, flicking it with my tongue until she's moaning uncontrollably.

"Please," she begs. "Please, I need—"

I stand abruptly, lifting her into my arms. She wraps her legs around my waist instinctively as I carry her to the bed.

"I need to be inside you," I growl. "Tonight, Aleksandr will sleep with us in this room. We won't get another opportunity to fuck."

I lay her down on the silk coverlet, her hair spreading around her like a golden halo. She looks up at me with trust and desire, her legs falling open in invitation.

I strip off my clothes quickly, my cock already hard and aching. She watches, her eyes darkening as she takes in my body.

"You're so big," she whispers.

I climb onto the bed, positioning myself between her thighs. "Have I ever told you I love taking you bare? Love feeling yoru softness smothering me."

I thrust inside in one hard stroke, filling her completely. She cries out, her nails digging into my shoulders.

"That's it," I groan. "Take me deeper. Let me feel you unprotected pussy clenching around me, begging for my seed."

I pull out and slam back in, setting a brutal pace. The bed creaks beneath us, the headboard thudding against the wall. Her breasts bounce with each thrust, and I lean down to suck one nipple into my mouth.

"Yes," she moans. "Harder."

I grip her thighs, spreading her wider, opening her up so I can go deeper. My thumb finds her clit, circling it firmly.

"Come for me," I demand. "Let me feel you squeeze my cock."

She explodes, her orgasm ripping through her. Her pussy clamps down on me rhythmically, milking me, and I can't hold back.

"I'm going to fill you," I growl. "Going to breed you until you're dripping."

I thrust deep one last time and come hard, my cock pulsing as I fill her with my seed. Wave after wave, until I'm empty and she's full.

I collapse beside her, both of us breathing hard. My hand moves to her stomach, patting it gently.

"You look the best when you're full of my cum," I murmur.

She laughs weakly. "You're insatiable."

"Only for you," I reply, pulling her close.

She curls into my chest, her hand resting over my heart. "I love you, Leo."

"I love you too, malishka."

TWENTY-SIX

Anya

I SPRITZ perfume at my wrists and behind my ears, the scent light and citrusy, expensive in a way that still feels unfamiliar on my skin. I don't need much. Leo notices everything anyway.

"Aleksandr," I say, reaching for my lipstick. "Be nice to the nanny, alright?"

He's perched on the edge of the bed, swinging his legs. "Where are you going?"

I smile at his reflection in the mirror. "I'm going to see Mr. Leo."

His face lights up instantly, like I flipped a switch. "Really?"

"Yes."

"Can I come too?"

I laugh softly. "No, it's a date."

He frowns. "What's a date?"

"It's when grown-ups talk about boring things," I say lightly. "You'd get bored."

"I don't mind," he insists. "Can I come?"

I cap the lipstick and turn to him. "Why do you like Leo so much?"

He shrugs. "I don't know. He's kind of cool."

I laugh again, warmer this time. "He is, isn't he?"

The realization hits me suddenly. We are both fangirling over the same man. It's ridiculous and unsettling and oddly sweet.

I brush my hair, slow and careful. Aleksandr doesn't leave. He lingers by the dresser, unusually talkative, asking questions about the perfume, the lipstick, why I don't dress the same as I used to when I was with his Papa. He used to be so quiet. Withdrawn. Petrov never encouraged his curiosity. He snapped at questions, treated them like inconveniences. Leo listens. Leo answers his questions, even when they're excessive or annoying. Aleksandr has started to come out of his shell by hanging around with Leo more. It's like he gets the confidence to be himself when he's around Leo. He used to hide himself away around Petrov, and even me.

Like every child, he could sense what his parents wanted him to be. And he played that role, afraid he'd lose our love if he didn't. Petrov wanted him to be quiet, and I wanted him to be empathetic, because I was too stressed with my marriage to focus on anything but the most mundane responsibilities. Perhaps neither of us really gave him the environment to show himself.

As I apply the final swipe of lipstick, I catch Aleksandr staring at me in the mirror.

"What?" I ask gently. "Do you like when I wear makeup?"

He hesitates. "Is Leo your boyfriend? Are you going to marry him?"

My hand slips. Just a little.

"No," I say too quickly. "It's not like that."

His shoulders droop. The disappointment on his face is sharp and immediate.

"He's just an old friend," I add. "Helping us. He'll be gone soon."

That makes it worse.

I gesture for him to come closer. He climbs onto my lap without protest, smaller than he should be for his age, still fitting there too easily. I wrap my arms around him.

"We'll be happy," I tell him. "Just you and me. We're visiting your grandparents this weekend, remember? We'll move in with them soon."

He wrinkles his nose. "I don't like their house. It's so cold in the winter. And it's always quiet. There's nothing to do around there."

I sigh. "I know. But the air is fresh."

He raises his head, eyes big and needy. "I want to stay in Moscow."

"We can't. I have to rent this apartment so we can have money to live."

"Can we stay with Leo, then? He has a big house."

"No," I say firmly. "Of course not."

The guilt hits immediately. I know my hometown will suffocate him. I know he needs space and noise and movement. But I have no income. I can't keep the apartment. Renting it out is the only way we survive.

Aleksandr puts his hands on my shoulders and looks at me seriously. Too seriously.

"Don't lie to me."

My breath catches. "Not lie about what?"

He swallows. "Is Leo my real dad?"

The room tilts.

"Why do you need to know that?" I ask carefully.

"Because I want to stay with him," he says. "And if he's my dad, I can."

His words shouldn't make me feel insecure. I know he's not trying to leave me for Leo. But it hurts nevertheless. To know that in such a short time, his bond with Leo surpasses his attachment to me.

I close my eyes for a second. "Even if Leo were your father, you couldn't stay with him."

"Why?"

"Because you're my son," I say, voice tightening. "We stay together."

His face scrunches, frustration spilling over. "I don't want to leave Moscow."

"It won't be so bad. You'll get used to the quiet. You'll make new friends. Besides, spending so much time around Leo isn't appropriate. You're getting too close to him," I snap. "He's not the right sort of man."

"That's not true," he fires back. "He's nice. He's rich, too. You just don't care what I want."

"That's not fair."

"You're forcing me to be what you need," he says, voice rising. "Not what I want to be."

I stand, heart pounding. "Leo is dangerous. He's not someone you should idolize."

"Then why do you invite him over?" he shouts. "Why do you smile when he's here?"

The words hit harder than I expect.

"I..." My words sputter out. I've been caught out in my own lie by my son. I keep telling myself Leo is dangerous, but I am drawn to him like a moth to a flame.

"You're a liar." Aleksandr's voice rises in pitch. "You are happy around him. And you don't want to admit it. I'm happy with him, too. But you don't care about that. You never left Papa even though he made us cry so much, but you want us to leave Mr. Leo who makes us happy. Do you even want the best for us?"

My throat stings. Hearing the truth spoken so plainly by a child is a different kind of experience. I know I clung to misery when I shouldn't have. I know I made the wrong decisions because I thought they'd keep me safe. I should have left Petrov earlier, but I never had the courage.

Maybe the problem is that I have too much pride. I keep resisting Leo, because I don't want to give him another chance to break my heart the way he did all those years ago. I'm scared of him growing distant from me like he did, making me feel useless and alone.

I'm still holding a grudge against him for something that happened years ago. My pride still doesn't want to take him back, even though he has proven so many times that he has changed.

Holding power over him, denying him the one thing he needs, makes me feel like I'm in control.

I lost any feeling of power after living with Petrov. Now I'm clinging to the illusion of control by hurting someone else.

"Of course I want the best for us," I tell him. "But I don't want to depend on someone else."

"Is it so bad to depend on someone else?" Aleksandr asks. "I'm a child."

He's right, of course. I used to be dependent on Petrov, too. But back then, I didn't feel the same. He cheated on me all the time, and I felt I was owed compensation. But I don't want to leech off Leo. I would feel like a burden if I did. And I have already taken too much from him.

Maybe I can get some kind of job in Moscow, though I don't know who'll hire me.

"I'm not leaving Moscow." Aleksandr marches to the door.

He storms out of the room, door slamming behind him.

I stand there, breathless, lipstick still in my hand, knowing he saw straight through me.

A WEEK LATER, I am visiting my parents alone.

I was supposed to come with Aleksandr, but he threw a tantrum this morning. ears, shaking hands, a refusal so absolute it startled me. He would not come with me. He locked himself in his room and told me he hated my hometown and hated my parents' house and hated that I never listened.

It was the first time he had ever spoken to me like that.

Since our fight, since I failed to deny that Leo was his real father, he has barely talked to me. Answers clipped. Eyes guarded. He is stubborn now in a way that feels new, sharpened by disappointment. I do not know how to reach him anymore.

In the end, I gave in. I left him at Leo's place. At least he grinned when he hugged Leo. It both hurt me and made me feel relieved. At least there's someone who can make him normal again.

The decision sits heavy in my chest as I walk through the small town where I grew up, my boots crunching softly against gravel and frost. The streets are narrow and quiet, lined with low houses and bare trees. Everything smells faintly of smoke and cold earth. Nothing has changed, and yet I feel like a stranger.

This is where I learned to skate on cracked outdoor ice. Where I walked to school with my skates slung over my shoulder. Where dreams felt both enormous and impossible.

My body feels off today. Heavy. My breasts ache, tender

beneath my sweater. I threw up earlier, barely managed to sip tea before nausea curled in my stomach again. I could not eat breakfast. It has been like this for a while now.

Stress, I tell myself.

The fighting. The distance. The guilt.

I have been dating Leo for two months. Two months of stolen laughter, quiet dinners, shared glances that say too much. Two months of reminding myself how it feels to be wanted, truly wanted. And still, I keep pushing him away.

Aleksandr's words echo in my head.

You're choosing unhappiness over happiness.

Leo is happiness. I know that now. He always was. The only man I ever loved. The only one who ever saw me clearly and still stayed.

Maybe it is time to stop pretending control is safety. Maybe it is time to let go of fear and accept that the future does not need to be certain to be worth living.

I have survived worse than uncertainty.

My parents' house comes into view, small and familiar, paint peeling at the edges. My mother opens the door before I even knock.

She looks older. They both do. My father's hair has thinned, his shoulders slightly stooped. My mother's hands tremble when she cups my face.

"My girl," she says softly. "You look tired."

"I am," I admit.

They make tea. We sit at the kitchen table where I once did homework, where my mother braided my hair before competitions. I already told them about my divorce, but not about my plans of moving back home. I do not tell them about the bruises or the fear or the nights I cried quietly so Aleksandr would not hear. Or what I'm trying to leave behind in Moscow by running away to my hometown.

Even the smell of my mother's piroshky makes my stomach churn with nausea. I don't touch it.

"I'm planning to move back with you," I say. "I have to rent the house in Moscow. It will bring in a steady income. I can pay for things around here."

My parents trade glances, looking concerned. "Here? Are you sure? The house is old."

"It's where I grew up," I reply.

"But it isn't where Aleksandr grew up," my mother says. "Will he like it here?"

My father frowns, echoing her sentiment. "Moscow is better for the boy."

My mother nods. "His education. His future.."

"I know," I say, pressing my fingers around the warm mug. "But I don't know if I can afford to stay."

"You used to be a champion," my mother says. "There must be some kind of job for you."

"And if I don't find one?"

"Then come home," my father says gently. "You know we'll always be here for you."

"Or we can move to Moscow. Take care of Aleksandr while you work," my mother adds.

"I have a nanny," I reply. Well, Leo is my nanny these days, but they don't have to know that. They don't even know I'm dating him.

They insist I stay the night. See if I can get used to the quiet again.

I laugh softly. "After years of hotels and guarded houses? I'll be fine."

That night, lying in my childhood bed, the ceiling unchanged, my phone buzzes.

Leo: *Did you get there safely?*

Leo: *I made him dinner. He pretended not to like it, then ate everything.*

I smile despite myself.

Leo: *He asked if horses sleep standing up.*

Leo: *I miss you.*

I type back slowly.

Anya: *Thank you for taking care of him.*

Anya: *I miss you too.*

The ache in my chest does not go away, but it softens.

The next day, my mother makes breakfast like she always does. Eggs, dark bread, butter cut into neat squares. The kitchen smells warm and familiar, comforting in a way that almost makes me cry.

I sit at the table and force myself to take a bite.

It barely makes it past my throat before my stomach turns.

I clap a hand over my mouth and rush to the sink. I do not even make it there. I retch, sharp and violent, my body folding in on itself as everything comes back up. My eyes water. My hands shake.

"Oh my God," my mother says, rushing to my side. She rubs my back, her palm warm through my sweater. "Anya, are you alright?"

I rinse my mouth and nod weakly. "It's just stress," I say. "Everything has been a lot lately."

She studies me the way only a mother can. Quiet. Watchful. Not convinced.

"You've barely eaten," she says. "You look pale."

"I'm fine," I insist, though even I can hear the doubt in my voice.

But when I sit back down and push the plate away untouched, a thought forms so clearly it makes my breath hitch.

This is not normal.

Two mornings in a row. The nausea. The soreness in my breasts. The strange exhaustion that feels deeper than sadness.

I think of Leo. Of his hands on my waist. Of the weeks we spent tangled together, reckless and hungry and finally honest. No protection. We never used condoms because I like him without any barriers, and I thought I was too old to get pregnant easily.

But I haven't hit my menopause yet, and there's probably still a few years to go before I do.

My pulse starts to race.

I leave my parents' house an hour later, hugging them goodbye, promising to call. The town feels smaller than ever as I walk to the station. The train rattles toward Moscow, the countryside blurring past the window, but I barely see it.

By the time I arrive, my hands are cold and damp.

I go straight to a pharmacy near the station. It smells of disinfectant and perfume. I keep my eyes down as I ask for the test, my voice steady despite the pounding in my chest.

Back at my apartment, I lock the door and sit on the edge of the bathtub.

I follow the instructions with care, my movements precise, almost reverent. Then I set the test on the sink and force myself to look away.

One minute feels like an hour.

When I finally turn back, my breath leaves me in a rush.

Positive.

I stare at it, frozen. Then I press a hand to my mouth as a laugh and a sob collide in my chest.

I am pregnant.

Leo's baby is growing inside me.

The shock gives way to warmth. To certainty. To a quiet, undeniable joy that settles deep in my bones. I am no longer confused. No longer split in two by fear and longing.

This is my answer.

I sink down onto the bathroom floor, my back against the tub, one hand resting over my belly. It is still flat. Still secret. But it already feels like everything.

I cannot lie to myself anymore. I love him. I want a future and a family with him. I want to have this baby, to give Aleksandr a sibling and to see my belly swell with Leo's seed.

And that means that I can't shut him out of my life anymore.

TWENTY-SEVEN

Leo

ALEKSANDR IS SITTING on the rug with Anechka, both of them bent over a pile of wooden blocks like it is serious business. He is explaining something to her with great authority, hands moving, voice animated. Anechka listens with wide eyes, nodding as if every word matters.

Aleksei lounges nearby, pretending not to watch them while absolutely watching them.

When the doorbell goes off, I wait for the guest I know is coming.

One of the foot soldiers accompanies Anya into the house.

Anya waves at me, her coat still on, her expression softer than it has been in days.

"Had a good night at your parents'?" I ask.

She smiles. "Yeah. And I see Aleksandr is in a better mood."

I look at her, puzzled. "He has been in a good mood since you dropped him off."

"Of course he has been. He is a different person around you." I sense something in her voice as she watches her son with equal parts awe and the kind of pain a parent feels while sending their kid to college. Her gaze moves to me, suddenly becoming more focused. "Can I talk to you for a second? In private."

I nod and lead her to my study, closing the door behind us. The room smells faintly of leather and old books. And oil and grease and metal, from all the guns I have hidden around here.

"Whiskey?" I ask automatically, already reaching for the bottle.

"No," she says quickly. "I can't. I'm pregnant."

I pause. Turn. Really look at her.

"Wait, what did you say? You're *pregnant*?" Disbelief crashes into sheer elation as I wonder if I made that up in my head. I have been breeding Anya, hoping to get her pregnant, but I never thought it would actually happen.

She takes a breath and reaches into her bag. When she places the pregnancy test on my desk, my mind refuses to catch up.

"I'm pregnant," she says.

The words land like a blow to my chest.

I stare at her. Then at the pregnancy test with two lines.

"Is this real?" My voice sounds distant to my own ears. "How long have you known?"

"I found out today."

I am across the room before I realize I have moved. I pull her into my arms, crushing her to my chest, my mouth finding hers in a kiss that is desperate and reverent all at once.

"Fuck, malishka," I whisper against her lips. "Is this actually happening?"

"Yes," she says, breathless. "I'm growing your baby, Leo."

Something flickers inside me. Joy. Awe. And then fear, sharp and immediate.

"What are you going to do?" I ask, hating myself for the question even as I need the answer. But I'm scared. Despite my best efforts, there's a wall between Anya and me. She has her boundaries, and respecting them is the only way I will be allowed to stay in her life. I can't order her around. She might leave immediately if I do.

"Are you going to keep the child?" I venture. She's over forty. The pregnancy might not be easy for her. Besides, I don't know if she wants to stay with me in the long-term, and she won't bring another child into the world unless she's certain.

She nods without hesitation. "I never thought about not having the child. I know I'm a bit older, but my first pregnancy was easy. I want another baby, Leo. I like being a mom. And I have always dreamed of having a daughter."

Relief crashes into me like a tidal wave. Thank goodness.

My breath leaves me in a rush. "Will you let me be a part of their life?" I ask. "I'll do whatever you want. Anything. I know you don't want Aleksandr to get close to me and you haven't decided if you want to be my wife—"

My words melt into silence. She steps closer and wraps her arms around me. "I decided when I saw the test. I want to be yours, Leo. I want us to be a real family this time. I want my kids to know you, to see your kindness, to grow up knowing what it feels like to be protected by someone strong."

Her voice breaks, and she starts to cry. I wipe away her tears, but fresh streams spill down her cheek.

"You know, Aleksandr and I argued last week." She sniffles. "He wants to stay in Moscow. He wants to move in with you. I admitted that you were his real dad. He really likes you. Even more than he likes me, I think. He has changed since he met you. He used to be so quiet, always shrinking himself, but now he's bright and vibrant."

"Anya..."

"Wait, let me finish." She hiccups, her sob cutting her sentence short. "He also told me that I clung to Petrov even though he made me unhappy, but I push you away even though you make me smile. And he was right."

"I was so angry with you," she continues. "When you neglected me and ignored me and broke up with me before, it bruised my pride. I felt like I had no control. I wanted you so badly, but I couldn't make you look at me anymore."

"I'm sorry," I say immediately. "I never meant to make you feel that way. I won't let that happen again."

She shakes her head. "People are allowed to have their own emotions. I used it as an excuse. An excuse to never take a real chance on love." She looks up at me, eyes wet but steady. "I told myself I was safer with Petrov, because I didn't love him. And if I never gave him my heart, he could never destroy me. Even when he disappointed me, it didn't hurt, because I expected nothing. The reason I clung to him was because I told myself not loving someone was the only way to keep myself safe."

I cup her face, my thumbs brushing away her tears.

"I know the future won't be easy," she continues. "But I'm ready to choose love. I have never loved anyone like I love you, Leo. I knew a long time ago that we're destined for each other. And not being together isn't easy. It isn't safe. It's torture."

I kiss her again, slower this time. "I want to make you feel safe," I murmur. "I want to erase everything he did to you."

She exhales. "Some of it was my fault. Not the abuse. Never that. But I should have left when he cheated. I should have married you then." She gives a shaky laugh. "I shouldn't have believed his lies, when he said he'd change."

She looks at me, really looks at me.

"But now," she says softly, "I'll accept your proposal."

I laugh, the sound breaking out of me before I can stop it. "You finally said yes after a decade. That might be the longest a man has ever waited."

She laughs too, through tears. "I love you," she says. "And I'm proud of you, proud of your strength and nobility. I think I'm a little proud of myself too. For choosing you."

I pull her into my arms and hold her there, my hand resting over her back, already imagining the life growing inside her.

"I promise," I say quietly, "I will make you the happiest wife in the world."

And for the first time in my life, I know exactly who I am fighting for.

EPILOGUE

Anya

THREE YEARS LATER...

MY DAUGHTER IS warm and heavy in my arms, her small fingers clutching at the soft knit of my sweater as if I might disappear if she lets go. Elena has Leo's eyes. That steady gray that seems too serious for a two-year-old and yet softens completely when she laughs.

She laughs now, high and bright, as Aleksandr races past with Anechka and Zorina's son in tow, their footsteps thundering across the marble floors of Zorina's mansion. I can't believe how much all the kids have grown. They're so big and noisy now, but it's happy noise.

The house is glowing. Candlelight, garlands, the scent of pine and spice and sugar. Christmas music hums quietly in the background, half drowned out by voices and laughter.

Lena is hosting us all again at her and Aleksei's townhouse for the annual family Christmas party. It's my fourth year joining this celebration, and it gets bigger and more extravagant every year. This year, Callista, Dmitry's wife, helped her plan the event. Since Callista is a professional event planner, the decorations look like something out of a magazine and the food is two notches up from the homely fare Lena usually serves.

"This is better than some of the food I've had at the Met Gala," Zorina nibbles on a canape. She's pregnant again, her stomach swollen with her second child. She's glowing, though. "You have to tell me the name of the caterer."

"I'll send it to you," Callista murmurs. She smiles at Elena whose eyes widen at her aunt's grin. "She's so cute." Callista taps her cheek. "She definitely takes after you."

I laugh. "I'm glad I had a daughter this time. I really wanted one."

"The bond between a mother and daughter is special," Callista agrees, looking at her own three-year-old daughter playing with her cousins.

I never imagined my life would look like this.

Lena presses a warm glass into my hand. "Mulled wine," she says with a knowing smile. "You deserve it."

I take it, grateful, the heat seeping into my palms. "Thank you."

Lena sits at the dining table with me and my other sisters-in-law. I have gotten to know all of them and they're like my own sisters now. Clara, Nikolai's wife, is a college student, but she's mature and smart for her age. Callista, an event planner, is ambitious and she always knows the best places to get everything, from baby clothes to expensive silverware. Lena is the soft, mother of the group, always bringing us together, planning girls' nights. And Zorina is the gossip and the rich aunt, spoiling our kids with lavish gifts and us with the latest gossip.

My life feels complete with them in it. Leo's love fills my heart, but my sisters feed my soul. I never had any siblings, and the relationship I have with these women feels special.

Lena watches Leo across the room, her expression thoughtful. "You know," she says, "he's changed. Since you married him. He used to be cold and distrustful. Now he's more relaxed, and fun to be around. The whole family feels different with you in it. Complete."

I shake my head gently. "It's the other way around. Leo made me softer. He completed me. I didn't even realize how guarded I was until I didn't have to be anymore."

Zorina hums in agreement. "That sounds like him. I trusted him the moment I saw him. He was scary, but dependable."

Callista sips her drink. "I'm just glad he took the pakhan position back," she says frankly. "Dmitry was drowning. He wouldn't admit it, but I could see it. He used to stay up all night, and look like a zombie in the morning. Leo must be superhuman for handling all that work alone and still looking human."

I laugh quietly. "Leo isn't superhuman."

Callista arches a brow. "Are you sure?"

I glance across the room. Leo has one hand on Aleksandr's back, steady and grounding, as Aleksandr talks animatedly about something he learned this week. Leo listens carefully, then makes a dry joke that has Aleksandr snorting with laughter. I love seeing their dynamic. It's something only men can have, and I no longer feel excluded. My relationship with Aleksandr is different, but it's also something Leo can't replicate.

Clara drifts over then, a playful spark in her eyes. "Monopoly," she announces. "It's tradition now."

I smile at that. Three years ago, I sat at a Christmas table like this, uncertain and half afraid, wondering if I belonged. I never imagined it would become home.

Nikolai appears at Clara's shoulder, grinning. "I call banker," he says. "And I refuse to apologize in advance."

"Of course you do," Lena mutters.

"Ladies," Nikolai adds with a wink, "you all look devastating tonight."

Elena squirms in my arms, reaching for Leo just as he comes up behind me. His hand settles on my shoulder, warm and familiar, and my entire body relaxes without conscious thought.

"I've got her," he says quietly, lifting Elena from my arms.

She curls into him instantly, as if she has always known where she belongs.

I watch him for a moment, my heart full to the point of ache. I have family now. Real family. Love that does not demand silence or endurance. Safety that does not come at the cost of myself.

When Leo looks back at me, his gaze steady and sure, I know with absolute certainty that I made the right choice.

I am no longer afraid.

I am where I was always destined to be.

ALSO BY KRYSTAL CLARK

Loved this book? Read how Nikolai, Dmitry, Aleksei, and Mikhail fell in love, starting with book #1 in the series, Aleksei and Lena's story, a full-length mafia romance with breeding, pregnancy, college romance, and more: Pregnant for the Bratva Dom

Want to know what's next? Subscribe to my newsletter to be informed of new book releases and read exclusive excerpts. I release at least one book a month. You can be the first to know about sales, free ebooks, and special offers.

If you like longer novels with instalove, breeding, pregnancy, and lactation, start reading this steamy series with the first book: Knocked Up by My Ex's Dad.

Love highly erotic short stories with milking/lactation kink? Check out Stalker Daddy's Milk.

Want to read more books this this, filled with taboo romance, forbidden love, and intense sex? Start with the first book in this series, Hucow for the Priest.

I have written more than 80 books with plenty of age gap, daddy kink, breeding, lactation, dark romance, mafia romance, hucow, and BDSM stories. Check out some of my other works!

Dark, sensual, spicy romances with an intense, consuming love story: Dominant Daddy's Captive Bride.

If you're eager for short cowboy romance novellas with breeding, and other kinks, start my cowboy romance series with: Baby-making

Like omegaverse erotica? Check out: Knot My Fated Mate

Alien's Omega Captive (MM)

Bully's Rejected Omega (MM)

Buy my box set collections, which contain 15 of my other books focused on breeding, daddy kink, and lactation.

Milky with Big Bellies

Taboo Daddy Short Stories Collection

Taboo Pregnant and Milked

And my other short stories:

Pregnant for My Alien Ex

Degraded by My Best Friend's Dad

If steamy monster romances with breeding kink, lactation, and pregnancy float your boat, try:

Maid for the Gargoyle Lord.

My Best Friend's Monster Dad

Kraken King's Bride

Arranged Marriage with a Werewolf

A Nanny for the Lich

Demon's Secret Baby

Milked by the Dragon

ABOUT THE AUTHOR

Krystal Clark is the author of over 100 erotica, contemporary romance, and monster romance books. Many of her books have been Amazon bestsellers in their categories. She writes hot and steamy stories with happy endings. She writes a variety of kinks, but her books often feature protective alpha males, lactation, pregnancy, and breeding kink. Get hooked to her addictive, high-heat romances today!

Printed in Dunstable, United Kingdom

77043323R00139